A
MILLION
QUIET
REVOLUTIONS

A
MILLION
QUIET
REVOLUTIONS

ROBIN GOW

FARRAR STRAUS GIROUX

NEW YORK

Farrar Straus Giroux Books for Young Readers
An imprint of Macmillan Publishing Group, LLC
120 Broadway, New York, NY 10271
fiercereads.com

Library of Congress Cataloging-in-Publication Data is available.

Printed in the United States of America
First edition, 2022
Book design by Liz Dresner

ISBN 978-0-374-38841-6 (hardcover)
10 9 8 7 6 5 4 3 2 1

For trans people
near, far, past, and future

CONTENTS

I

NAMES

NAMES

We let go of our names together
on the same night.

You sleep over and I play
the portable vinyl player my parents

got me for my seventeenth birthday.
It's blue and slick like the hood of a retro car.

I only have one record and it's my dad's old Beatles album
Yellow Submarine.

We listen for hours on repeat,
talking and talking about summer ending,
and we start listing all the beautiful things we'll miss:

kissing behind the crooked tombstone in the graveyard at dusk,
cheese fries at the snack shack,
filling Tupperware with fireflies.

You give me a rainbow pin
for my backpack and show me
your own matching one.

You say, "If anyone asks
you can say you just like those colors."

Even though the door is shut
you're still shy as you put your arm
around me in my new queen-sized bed.

I miss lying with you in the bunk bed,
now moved to the attic.

The bunk bed was more . . .
I don't know . . .
romantic, maybe.

We don't want to ruin the sleepovers
by letting anyone know that we're dating.

We're talking about getting coffee at
the diner on Main Street and all of
a sudden you say, "The word *lesbian*
sounds mythical, like a dragon or a siren . . .
I don't know how I feel about calling myself that.
The word just feels
wrong for me."

I say, "I know what you mean."

You look stunning in your new/not-new jean vest
and red T-shirt with the space rover on it
that we just got from Goodwill.

I put on my pajamas:
a soft white tank top and polka-dot shorts.

You turn over and rest your head
on my chest. You kiss my clavicle.

"Can I ask you something?"

"Of course," I say, scared
that you don't love me anymore
and that the summer is going to be over
and never ever come back.

"I think I want to buy a chest binder.
You can get them online.
Sometimes for only like thirty bucks."

You stand up and brush your hands
over your chest.
"They'll be flat, like
more than a sports bra."

"How are you going to order it?" I ask.

"I have one of those Visa gift cards
I got from CVS."

"Oh, okay."

I'm burning jealous. I didn't know
until now how much I want one, too.

I've read about them on Tumblr
but never seen one in person.

"And I want to send it to your house
because . . . my parents can't find it."

"Of course," I say, knowing
that my parents never remember to get packages.
"I've thought about getting one, too."

You pause, surveying me
in the gentle way you do, the way
a pool of water might look
at someone.

"Do you not want me to, like . . .
touch your boobs anymore?" you ask,
and I laugh.

"Yeah, maybe not anymore."

"Same for me," you say.

You roll over and
look at my pastel-pink ceiling fan.

"One more thing," you say.
"I don't want you to call me [****] anymore."

"What should I call you?"

"I don't know yet."

I see your old name like a moth,
dusty-winged and glowing.

The name escapes out the
open window and into the soupy
August night,
into forever.

I sit up and cup my hands.

"What are you doing?" you ask.

"I want to let mine go too," I say.

YOU

On the first day
of first grade

you were the only kid who was dressed nice
in a white button-up shirt and dressy tan pants
like something we would wear to synagogue

only you don't go to synagogue,
you go to church, actually specifically
you go to mass, which you tell
me is different from church
but also seems still pretty much
the same idea as synagogue.

You were worried about getting
dirty on the playground with your
nice clothes

so we walked and collected caterpillars
under the big oak tree.

I told you that I was from Hawaii
because I thought it sounded more
interesting than being from
up the street.

You said you were
from Puerto Rico and
I didn't know where that was.

You said you had a brother
named José
and I was jealous because
I didn't have any siblings.

AS WE GOT OLDER I NOTED ALL THE THINGS I MORE-THAN-LIKE ABOUT YOU:

1. Your excitement when you draw a new character.

Now that we have phones you just
text me pictures but when
we were little you'd call the house phone
and describe your drawings to me, saying

"And his arms are really bright blue
and his eyes are brown and he can shoot
fire from his eyes."

2. The way you hoist yourself and me up into the trees in the park.

I stay on the low branches as
you climb higher.

Your brother
taught you how to climb trees.

When the two of you were both little
you'd try to climb to see if
you could talk to God,

shouting at the clear sky,
trying to get through to him.

3. The way you watch me bake banana bread and always crack
   the eggs just right.

I can never do it.

I used to be the "egg cracker" for Mom when she'd bake but
I'm always too gentle.

I push the shell slowly until it gives
so tiny flecks of shell always
end up in the batter.

You don't hesitate,
a steady flick of the wrist,
a clean fracture of the shell.

FIRST AND SECOND KISS

I was technically your second kiss
even though you say you really think of me as your first.

Jackson Williams was your technical first kiss
at the park in the summer before fifth grade.

We were all doing dares, a bunch of kids from town
and you and me. Jackson dared you to kiss him,

so you did. You said it was squishy and awful.
Really, I think a first kiss can only count

if it's not a dare or it's with someone you like.
The next day we were alone by the creek

and you asked me, "Will you dare me to kiss you?"
I said, "I dare you,"

and you kissed me longer than a dare kiss.
We were quiet after and then kept talking

as if it hadn't happened.

TEXT MESSAGE FROM YOU

I can't hang out tonight ☹
I have youth group at church.

Mom would destroy me
if I tried to get out of it.

Maybe tomorrow?

You haven't told anyone
we're together, right?

I keep worrying Mom already knows somehow.
I swear moms know everything.

Me:

Don't worry!
I'd never tell anyone. I promise.

ME

Our house is quiet
and we don't use the television.

Most nights you can find me
and Mom and Dad sitting
in the living room all reading books.

Dad reads books about history.

Mom reads books with stories
and sometimes books of poetry.

Dad says he could never read poetry.

"It doesn't make any sense."

Sometimes Mom will read a poem aloud.

My favorite poems are
the ones that don't make sense.

I read fantasy books
and sometimes mysteries.

I also read about
history like Dad, but different history.

Last year I was into ancient history,
especially Greece and Rome.

I know that it was standard back then
but I loved that men wore dresses.

The idea
excited me.

To me it meant that
people dressed differently and
maybe someday it'll change again.

This year it's the American Revolution.

I have to be honest, I got into it because
I loved that men dressed so fancy during the 1700s.
They wore wigs and heels—how fun is that?

As I read more, though,
I'm interested in how differently they thought
about war back then.

What did it mean to stand in rows
and take aim?

How did they understand being
American?

ONLY CHILD

Sometimes I'm jealous
of your big brother, José.

I guess if I had a sibling, I might feel differently.
You're always rolling your eyes
when I ask if you could
invite José to join us
when we hang out.

You say, "He's like practically an adult,
he doesn't want to chill with us."

I'd never tell you
but I think José is cool.

I know it's super weird
but when I was figuring stuff out
about being a boy

I thought
a lot about José.

He's the kind of man I want to be.

He plants basil by the side of your house.

He cooks instant oatmeal for afternoon snacks.

He writes little poems for you and leaves them in your shoes.

He's the kind of boy everyone should want to be.

KUTZTOWN

We talk all the time
about moving away,

but sometimes I wonder
if we'd miss Kutztown.

Not the people,
but the sprawling fields
and patches of forest
between farms.

I think I would miss
the cows.

How they lie down
before a rainstorm.

I do think we need a coffee shop, though.
Ever since the diner on Main Street closed
we've had to get

drinks at the Malt Shoppe:
melting blue slushies
and thick clumpy milkshakes.

Kutztown is boring.

There's no one like
us in Kutztown.

I feel lonely in Kutztown,

even when it's
me and you

looking down Main Street
in the summer and debating
whether or not to
go to the thrift shop
for the second time
in a week.

I would miss the market, though,
that's for sure.

Wooden baskets of apples
and warm doughnuts in glass cases.
Your favorite treat there
is the apricot scones.

If we moved away
I'd have to learn how
to bake them for you.

FOLK FESTIVAL

Every summer the Kutztown Folk Festival comes
to the fairgrounds across town with

the smells of fried blooming onion and fresh kettle corn
and the sounds of fiddles and folk songs.

There are all kinds of dancing
and theater and hit-and-miss engines
and snack shacks and wooden toys
and baking contests.

Basically, all the high schoolers work there in the summer.
This past year, you and me
worked at stands across from each other on the fairway.
Me at the ox roast stand
and you at the apple pie booth.
(I always wished we could switch.)
I was probably the first and only vegetarian
to work at the ox roast stand.
(Why didn't we get a say in which stands we worked?)

We walked home together each day,
only holding hands
after we were far away from the festival.
We would look around the fairgrounds each day
and see straight couples of all ages—
an old man feeding his wife
a greasy home fry, a couple we knew from school
climbing the hay bales together—
and we'd know we couldn't do that.
Not yet. Once

I grabbed your hand by accident
and in the few seconds we held hands after our shifts
a man walking past saw us.
He stared and stared and stared. We walked a foot apart
the rest of the way out of the fairgrounds.

Later, you told me, "We should be more careful."
I told you I agreed, but alone in my room I cried.
I didn't want to feel
so scared.

MALT SHOPPE

I guess I would miss the Malt Shoppe, too,
if we moved away from Kutztown.

It has red-and-white checker-patterned walls
and spills 1950s hits from its chrome door.

On a really crowded night in July
sometimes I felt like no one would notice us

or maybe they'd just think we were two close friends
splitting a sundae and sitting across from each other

at one of the red booths.
We'd ask for two cherries on top of our sundae

and race to try to tie the stems inside our mouths.
You could always do it—

holding up your little knotted stem
as I laughed and gave up.

HISTORY

You say you don't like history
because there's never anything about people like us.

In Mr. Claus's Senior Honors US History class,
the whole first week, I watch you spend class playing *Call of Duty*
on your laptop with the other boys.

You share glances across the room,

a silent code language you have for war.

It scares me to imagine you really in World War II
like the digital men you embody.

I see you:
face caked in dirt,
olive-green uniform,
the distant drumming of
machine-gun fire.

I hate the idea that war could be a game,
but I love when you win.

No one has ever offered to share the game download
with me.

I don't want to play
or even know how,

but I want to be seen as a boy
like how they see you.

I'm not sure how anyone wins at *Call of Duty*
but I know when you win
you bite your lip

and clench your fist tightly against the desk in triumph.

YOU TALK ABOUT BEING AMERICAN

You tell me,

> "It doesn't feel like it means anything
> to be American.
> It's like naming the color of air.

I don't feel American.
Maybe that's why I can play *Call of Duty*.

It doesn't feel like me.
It doesn't feel real.

Maybe it's not that I don't feel American
but more like America doesn't feel like me.

What is American?
Fourth of July? Red, white, and blue?
Apple pie? Burgers?
Red pickup trucks? Corn on the cob?
Frozen TV dinners?

I'm not any of those things.
In my heart
I think of Puerto Rico as my home
but sometimes my island
feels like a far-off dream.

And Puerto Rico is America.
But America is not Puerto Rico.
It's a stolen land.
First Spain, then the United States.

How can I even begin
to unravel what that means?"

HISTORY CLASS

At Kutztown, usually, every year we just cover
US History over and over,

as if each year, in early September, time whirls back to the 16th
century.

We all get sick with yellow fever.
We all go hungry in the winter.

Those in Roanoke disappear mysteriously.

Bodies summoned in the pages of an old textbook
that smells off-white.

This year, we were caught by surprise
when Mr. Claus started off class with the First World War
and explained that we would be studying up till the 1990s.

Right now, my favorite era is the Revolution, mostly because
no one else I know
likes to learn about it anymore—

they think we've talked about it
too much in school already.

Either that or they don't focus on
the same aspects I like to. They see it as
this one American triumph or something

when really I see the Revolution as much messier
than we make it seem.

Even all the people in the colonies didn't agree with it
and that's not even getting into
what it was like to live as someone
other than a
white
Protestant
land-owning
man.

WORLD WAR II

Dad likes World War II,
but he only really reads about the machines,
like guns and tanks.

Sometimes I think he likes reading
about weapons because they seem
distanced from the actual battlefields
where people were hurt and
where people died.

Maybe even more distant
still from places outside
the battles where people died.

I read about the Holocaust
in one of his books
last year.

I told Dad.

He said
he didn't want to talk about
that part.

Mom says that's because
it doesn't feel like
history to him.

His grandparents,
my great-grandparents,
were survivors
of the Holocaust.

He even
gets *World War Two Magazine*.

All the issues are stacked
on the little cabinet in the downstairs bathroom.

I page through them occasionally,
but just for the images painted
on the sides of fighter planes.

They're mostly images of half-naked ladies.

I don't look at them like THAT.

I look at them and think, *Why would you*
want the thing that drops a bomb
to be painted with a naked woman?

THE AMERICAN REVOLUTION

I got interested in the American Revolution
first when I was younger

because Dad and I used to take hikes
at Valley Forge.

When he was in high school,
he did reenactments there,
living in one of the cabins
soldiers had stayed in over a hundred years ago.

He'd show me the bunks the same size
as the ones men had slept in, and
I'd crawl in and claim that I'd have loved
to be a soldier back then.

He'd try to explain that it was winter
and they didn't have heaters but I was still
just excited by the cannons poised around the park
and the little houses scattered around
the rolling grass hills.

I imagined being a soldier there
with you and me sharing a bunk together.

We were in elementary school then,
so I just thought of us as close friends
out in the war together.

I considered how we might
combine our rations and have
meals together—how we might
get to see each other on Sundays and holidays
(when the generals gave soldiers time off).
I wondered
if any men celebrated Chanukkah or
anything other than Christmas. I'd only ever seen
paintings of Valley Forge soldiers on Christmas.

I've been thinking about Valley Forge
a lot lately
with all the books I've been reading.

I think about how all these soldiers
held this place all winter
through snow and ice.

I'm terrified that people
could ever want to go through that
for the idea of a country. I don't think
I would be able to survive that.

What did they think they were fighting for
and who did they think they were fighting for?

Did they fall in love with each other?

Did they fall in love with the idea of a country?

One of the books I was reading
talked about how Native American groups
made choices to align themselves with
the Americans or the British
in attempts to preserve whatever land they could,

and I'm reminded that the colonists were
fighting for land that wasn't even theirs to begin with.

There are all these threads to the Revolution
that cross for me at Valley Forge—

in the frozen Pennsylvania woods
where men waited in fear
of ambush.

VALLEY FORGE

I
tell you
about Valley Forge
because I hope it will
get you to see why I like

history so much. The story doesn't
impress you when I tell you at lunch.
You eat the same peanut butter and

fluff sandwich you have since first grade. Recently
you started liking plain baked chips. I watch as you slip
a few chips onto the potato roll. I eat hummus and pita chips;

it's been my most recent kick. We change the subject from history
to comic books. You're writing one and you show me some of the test

frames. It's about two superheroes
who are trans boys. They have the power

to move through time and they fight for queer people in the past
and the present and the future. You read to me and when you're done
you pause and say,

"It's not that I don't like history—it's just that in history class . . .
all of school, really . . . there's never anything

about people like us . . .
so I want to write stories
that show we exist."

PEOPLE LIKE US?

It's hard to search
for someone like yourself
when you're not even sure
who you are.

The word *transgender* sounds clinical, like
"Nurse! Apply the transgender!"

and the word *trans* dangles out there
like a raft drifting farther and farther away
from everything I've ever been taught
about gender.

I search *trans, the prefix*
and the dictionary says the word can mean

"across" and "beyond" and "through" and "changing thoroughly"

all of which are things lots of people in high school seem to be
but especially "changing thoroughly."

I wonder what makes this change different.

I wonder why it has to be me and

somewhere deep in my core

I think how wildly beautiful it
is to exist in spite
of all the places the stories

of men like you, like us, are
left untold.

"ACROSS"

We cross the creek behind your house
on Friday afternoons,

balancing ourselves on our little log bridge.
We built the bridge first two summers ago
and rebuild it each time the log is carried away
by a thunderstorm or sudden downpour.

We don't talk until we get deep enough in the woods
that you're no longer afraid
your parents will hear us
or see us if we kiss and hold each other.

"I don't know if I'll ever tell them,"
you say, and it breaks my heart.

I say, "Maybe someday they'll come around."

And I feel wrong for saying that because
I know your parents and
you say it can be hard to talk to them.

"They have enough going on with José.
I don't need to add to it."

"Well, José isn't your problem."

"It's awful, though. It's awful.
He just doesn't talk anymore.
He goes about his business but he won't say anything . . .

I don't think they would have noticed if
he hadn't started hiding so he could skip church."

"That's . . . that doesn't make sense.
José wanted to be a priest . . . Isn't he twenty now?"

You just nod.

We let the quiet of
the forest nestle between us.

In the trees some birds flutter and call.
I hear the distinct scratching sound
of squirrels climbing higher.

"I'm going to start making
a list of names," you say.

"There's so many,
I don't know how I'll ever pick one," I say.

"Maybe I won't change my name at all," you say.

"I've seen some trans people
just change their pronouns."

After a pause you continue.

"But I want a better name . . .
one that feels mine."

I think about your parents
and I wonder
why they chose the name you have—

think about how it can feel hard
to part with a birth name
even if it's what we need.

YOUR PARENTS

Your parents don't
ask if I want to come inside
when we walk home together.

They always used to, when we'd
walk in with a whole troop
of kids after school.

Your mom would ask, "Are you hungry?
Are you hungry?" to every one of us.

I think they don't like me anymore
but I might just be reading too much into things.
Sometimes I worry I make everyone's lives
more complicated—but especially yours.

I tell you this as we amble through the last
embers of summer in the woods, trying not
to remember that we're back in school.

We keep saying, "Seniors, can
you believe we're seniors?"

"I think they're just dealing
with a lot right now," you say,

and I wonder
if you're just trying
to make me feel less worried.

I search myself,
wondering what I might have said
to make them distrust me.

"It's not you.
They just wish that I did more family
stuff like I used to.
They care a lot about mass and, you know,
you don't go to mass, which I don't
care about but maybe they do.
I also used to have more friends,
maybe they just want me to have
lots of friends.
Sometimes I'm not sure what I can do
to make them happy."

"I wish we had more friends
too sometimes . . . Not that you're
not enough . . . just sometimes
I wish there were more kids like us."

"There are, maybe, just not here," you say.

At home at night I wonder
what church is like for Catholics.

I wonder what they think
of "people like us."

I imagine gold
and chalices and a big wooden cross

and your whole family drinking wine
and eating bread around
a table.

TWO OF YOU

Near the end of the walk you say,

"Sometimes I feel like there are two of me.
One who is a good *hija*.

She helps Mom cook. She does what she's told.
She gets perfect grades.

She is going to be a nurse
just like Mom.

I think of the picture of me
in my white First Communion dress.

The other me is bold and queer.
He has hair dyed red.

He wraps himself in a trans flag.
He doesn't care what his family thinks.

I don't know who I am sometimes between
the two of me

or what it would look like
for those two mes
to come together."

HOLY GUARDIAN ANGELS

When I was little, I was really
scared of your church.

It's a huge tall building
with amber-colored stained-glass panes
across the front.

I used to think they looked
            like big glossy scabs
or the shells of beetles.

            I know it seems silly now
but I was also scared of
            what Catholics do at mass

after that one day
            I overheard your mom talking
about "body and blood."

            I imagined it was some secret ritual
that only Catholics could know
            the details about.

It didn't help that you
            told me how much you hated it,

especially having to
            sit on those benches for so long.

I remember you rushing up
            to me one Monday morning
to tell me about

            how the priest had
talked about masturbation
            and how it's a sin.

I laughed but back at home
            I worried that there might actually
be something wrong with touching myself

            so I stopped for a month or so.

YOU TALK ABOUT ANGELS

You say,

> "I hate church but I do like angels.
> I think if anything is real it's probably angels.
>
> Mom has a picture of three angels
> tacked above my bed
> from when I was little.
>
> I always noticed how they
> had the same skin color as me.
>
> Even Our Lady of Providence,
> the patroness of Puerto Rico,
> is always super pale.
>
> I imagined in heaven
> there might be angels of all skin tones
> even if they weren't always recognized
> on Earth."

HELL

I don't believe
in hell.

I think people who do
get so hung up on not going there

that they forget all the
wonderful things happening on Earth.

I don't think that I believe
in heaven, either, to be honest.

All the time

you joke and list for
me all the reasons

you're going to hell.

I pretend that it's funny
because you also pretend
that it's funny.

You laugh at the things
that hurt you most.

You say, "I'm gay, so I'm going to hell."

"I watch porn, so I'm going to hell."

"I masturbate, so I'm going to hell."

"Remember when we
went to the dollar store last week?"

I nod.

"Yep, I stole a Crunch bar.
I'm going to hell."

Instead of laughing

I just want to tell
you that all those things
                    (well, except for stealing the Crunch bar,
                    which was stupid)

should be normal.

SYNAGOGUE

We go to
the Reform Congregation Oheb Sholom.
Like I told you, there's all different
types of synagogues,
just like there are different
kinds of churches.

But since
I've gotten older

and Mom took on more work
at the office

and Dad started another factory weekend shift,

we go less.

I had my bat mitzvah
five years ago, but it feels
like just this afternoon.

It's pretty much the same for boys
and girls.

I wonder if I'll have to redo it all

if/when I tell my parents.

The thought of
having a bar mitzvah excites me,
the whole community
getting together to see me
how I see myself.

I don't know if I believe in God
but I guess I would want him
to see me for who I am too

but then

I wonder if the other families
and the Rabbi
would let me do my bar mitzvah
at synagogue,

if they would see me as a man
someday.

A MAN SOMEDAY

The word *man* is heavy.
It makes me think of bodybuilders
and fathers.

I imagine stones under
their muscles, peeling back
the skin to reveal that
all men are really
made of granite and
sometimes limestone
and only very rarely metals:
hunks of
silver and copper under skin.

I prefer the word *boy*
for right now. It reminds
me of rubber balls and
blue caps and outfields
and bow ties.

I don't know if I'll
ever be heavy enough to
call myself a *man*.

I want to ask you
if you ever feel like this
but I'm scared that it
will make me seem less real.

A JEWISH MAN SOMEDAY

Even though I've always been taught men and women are equal
    in Judaism,
I've always known there are differences.

There are even different words for *bar* and *bat* mitzvah
and most other roles. I know it's just the language
but it bothers me.

It's complicated because
the words and the traditions feel so important
to who I am.

I've never felt really at home in Kutztown
but I've always been supported by my synagogue.

I don't want that to change.

Still, it's hard to make sense of everything about gender.

Can you fault people in the past
for not imagining that sex and gender could be separate?

And gender can be so beautiful in Judaism.
I felt so loved at my bat mitzvah.

Sometimes it doesn't feel right
to just move from one gender to the other.

I feel exactly how you put it—
I feel like there's two of me sometimes.

It feels like I'd have so much to learn
if I wanted to be a Jewish man and yet so much
about being a Jewish man would mean
having more privilege and authority than being a woman.

I feel like I'd be leaving a part of myself behind.

REAL

What makes someone real?

I think it has something
to do with touching.

When I touch you I feel real.

I feel like with your hands
moving over my skin
you are making my body

and I am making yours.

I think I could survive
if no one else ever saw me
as a boy as long as

at night in bed we could
kiss.

We've never gotten
undressed before but
I imagine it

all different ways.

I've never seen trans men
have sex.

This is exciting.

Would you have a blue dick
emerging from your backpack
to become part of our bodies?

Would you move your hand
forward and back,

calling my parts
a dick, transformed

in your hands?

NOT REAL

I've been thinking about all the ways
the world makes us feel
NOT real. I think people imagine
    transphobia and queerphobia as
people shouting at us and hurting us, which of course it is
    sometimes,
but really mostly at school and in town
I feel like people are trying to erase us—
like they just don't want to see us,

              which is
just another type of violence.

Like how at Kutztown everyone needs to bring
an "opposite sex" date to prom. People go as friends, sure,
but it's still like subtly saying "being queer isn't real"
or "all that matters is being hetero."

Then, like, even gym class. Why do we have
a different gym class for girls and for guys?

Where do we fit in? I don't want to be with girls
but I also know high school boys can be pretty cruel.
And in the locker room
it's not like anyone says aloud that they want to avoid me
but everyone congregates on the other side.
I pick a locker in the back because I'm scared.
I feel safer just alone back there. I feel like
the only way to exist as a queer person here
is to hide.

BEFORE THE REVOLUTION,

when I was into Greece and Rome,
sometimes I'd imagine the locker room
as the entrance to one of the great bathhouses in Athens.

They used to have these huge stone buildings
where everyone would gather and bathe together.
I know it sounds a little weird
but I like to imagine it as healing, everyone
accepting each other's bodies. I almost don't care
if that was how it really was, which I guess makes me
a bad historian.

Back when I'd picture this, I still didn't know I was a boy,
so I'd invent a story for myself. Maybe I was
a scholar woman, taking a break in the day
between writing stories or reading scrolls.
I didn't do as much research then.
I guess it was more fantasy than history but it was
what I needed—it helped me feel that
there wasn't something wrong with me,
that there was just something wrong
with this time in the world.

Thinking back, though, it is kind of funny.
Our grimy locker room is far from
a luxurious bathhouse.

"BEYOND"

Saturday I'm thinking that maybe
I can go back, that maybe
all these thoughts of being
a boy or a man or whatever

are just nonsense.

What you said about
history ripples through me and
I can't stop hearing

there's never anything
about people like us

there's never anything
about people like us

there's never anything
about people like us

It's like the wind is chanting,
but all of a sudden, I hear it differently.

There's never anything
written down
about people like us.

And I think of your comics and
I tell myself that we were there.

We have to have been.

"THROUGH"

Saturday night I tumble into the internet
like I do most nights I'm not spending with you.

I click article after article
on the Revolution. I learn about generals
and mercenaries and the kind of gear
the soldiers might have had.

I get bored and decide to just type in *Gay Revolutionary War*
and the first article is about
a head general who was openly gay
in a time when homosexual "activity" was illegal.

I mean, from what I can tell it's not like
he had a pride flag, but there weren't any pride flags back then.

I'm excited. I stand up from my desk.
It's such a small detail to most people but
to me the idea that people discovered this person's queerness
all these years later makes me think

that there are pieces of us not forgotten—
that there's some sort of channel of queer history
embedded in us waiting to be unearthed.

DOWN THE RABBIT HOLE

I jump to another article that comes up
as suggested at the bottom
about women who
joined the Continental Army.
I click on it
sort of aimlessly.

The image at the top is of a person crouched and binding their
    chest,
hiding behind a bush during battle,
getting ready
to put on their uniform.

They look so much
like how trans men bind their chests today
that I start to get this idea:

What if there were

two soldiers,
two men,

just like us—
all the way back then?

If these women could be seen as men
then maybe men like us
really did—really could have existed.

I WANT TO FIND MORE.

I scroll to the comments section on the article,
hoping for some other fragment of information.

There are dozens of trolls making jokes
about the image of the person binding their chest
and a few more comments by other history buffs
just saying how cool the article is.

At the very bottom, though, there's
a link to a Twitter thread—

I click and it's dozens of posts long.

QUEER REVOLUTIONARY
LOVE STORY: A THREAD

*Just as a disclaimer I'm not a history person or anything
but I am trans and I thought
this might help other people out there feeling alone*
1/9

I totally forgot about this until like literally today
but I was sitting around wishing I could find a story
about trans men in history and I remembered this . . .
2/9

When I was in middle school my class went on a tour
of our tiny historical society. It was mostly SUPER boring
but the tour guide was fun and told us a bunch of local history
      stories.
3/9

One story was about how female soldiers who fought in the
      Revolution
would find each other. The guide said
they would share tricks for how to pass as men—as soldiers.
They would help and take care of each other.
4/9

The tour guide said some of them even took women lovers.
She didn't say anything about trans people
probably because I imagine society
didn't really know what trans people were
or even have any idea that was possible.
These two who lived in my town
were supposedly named Aaron and Oliver.
5/9

They helped each other forge documents
and performed so well in the army that no one
would dare question their "manliness" or whatever.
6/9

When they returned from the war
they told people they were brothers and they lived together
in Royersford, Pennsylvania.
7/9

The tour guide said people only figured out
they were assigned female at birth
after they died (because of the autopsy or whatever).
I can't find anything about it online
but idk it sounds possible
to me.
8/9

What do you all think?
Have you ever heard of this story before?
9/9

MAYBE NO ONE EVER KNEW

Maybe two men like us met and
loved each other.

I take screenshots of the thread.
I have to show this to you.

Oliver and Aaron.

What if they met
in a cabin in Valley Forge
and made it through the winter together?

I love them so much—
I have to tell you about them.

I wonder if you'll understand—
if you'll think this article is
as important as I do.

I'm worried you won't think
the story in the comments is real.

The truth is,
I don't care if it's real.

We've been erased from
so much history.
Someone needs
to write us back in.

"CHANGING THOROUGHLY"?

I hold the story to myself a whole week
and my other secret, that I'm a boy, along with it.

I feel like I'm floating,
living without a name.

I feel like I can keep going because
I'm carrying these men with me.

I see them holding hands in uniform
on the corner of my street as I walk to school.

It turns out to be just two saplings a neighbor planted.

History class pushes time forward.
The First World War is ending and we're
over a hundred years away from
the Revolution.

We study together and memorize causes of the war for an essay
that will be on the test:

1. Assassination of Archduke Franz Ferdinand
2. Mutual Defense Alliances
3. Imperialism
4. Militarism
5. Nationalism

It occurs to me that the only thing I know about this man
Archduke Franz Ferdinand

is that he was assassinated.

Who did he love?

Maybe he sometimes watched
a man pass by him and

thought that in another world
they might be allowed to love each other.

Maybe not. But still maybe.

IN MY HEAD

sometimes I pretend to be one of the soldiers.
I pretend school is really an academy we need to finish
before we can go off to war.

I know this isn't really how the Revolution worked
but I'm sure they had some sort of camps
to practice drills and learn formations.

When we pass each other in the halls
I think about how impossible it must have felt at first
for the soldiers to discover they loved each other.

There was no word like *gay* or *straight*
and especially not *trans*. That's why
I kind of like *queer* to describe

LGBTQIA+ people from different times.
Queer says there's so much room
to explore uniqueness. Says there are so many ways

to exist. I also start to think
about how long it took for us to realize
we were more than just friends. It's like

our story runs alongside the soldiers' story
and all the other stories in between
of trans people falling in love with trans people.

WE'RE "CHANGING THOROUGHLY"

I tell myself that
I have to come out to my parents soon,
that I can't keep holding this.

Sometimes my mom can tell I'm keeping
something from her and Dad
and she asks, "What is wrong, honey, what's going on?"

I say "nothing" so many times
it becomes an automatic response to whenever
she starts to speak.

"Should we get pizza tonight?"
"Nothing."

She looks up from her phone.

"[****], tell me what's going on . . . Are you okay?"

I say nothing and bury my face in my hands.

I don't want to look at her.

I start crying like I never have.
It's just like sticking a knife in a water bottle.

I have practiced many times
how I would tell my mother I'm a boy
but that rehearsal goes
out the window and language fails me.

"Oh, baby, what's wrong?" she asks. "If you're gay, that's okay . . .
    we know," she says.

Dad comes into the room.

I haven't even imagined coming out to him,
at least not yet.

Somehow in all of it I tell them.

I say it all broken. I say

"I'm sorry" but then I say "I'm a man"

and "I love you."

                    and "I'm a boy."

They both hold me.

They are confused but not upset.

All they say is that they love me
and we don't talk more
about it.

I think about you
and hope your parents will hold you

someday like mine did
when you tell them.

QUESTIONS

My mom texts me questions,
about last night.

She waits until I leave the house for school
and on the walk to school we text

which is funny because

I usually text you on the way to school.

I forget what day it is.

It's a Thursday.

One more day till we sleep over
and I can tell you everything.

Mommy: Are you transgender?

Me: yes, i think so

Mommy: We love you, you know that?

Me: yes

Mommy: Dad says he loves you, too

Me: thnx

Mommy: Should we get you a meeting with a therapist?

Me: i dont know

Mommy: Okay!

Mommy: Do you have a name in mind?

Me: not yet this is new

Mommy: okay!

Mommy: Maybe we can help you find a name?

Me: maybe
(What I mean is that I don't want them to help . . . I want to
    pick my own name.)

Mommy: We had ideas already if you were a boy!

Me: okay, talk later?

Mommy: Okay!

Mommy: Do you think you're going to want . . . the treatments?

Me: Hormones? Surgery?

Mommy: Any of that?

Me: i just dont know mom, pls it's a lot

im still figuring it out

(That's what I say but what I mean is that I want to talk to you
    because
you're the only one who will understand.)

STILL "CHANGING THOROUGHLY"

Friday we sleep over and I tell you everything.

I start
with Oliver and Aaron.

I'm worried you won't think it's a story about us—
my hands shake.

I worry that you'll think it's just another
one of my history stories I ramble
on about

but you do
you hear me

and you wrap your arms around me as we lie
on the top bunk of my old bunk bed in the attic.

We decided to have our
sleepover up there this time for a change.

I think about how the bunk bed is similar to the bunks
soldiers in the Revolutionary War might have stayed in
at Valley Forge. Well . . .
mine is more comfortable
than straw, wood, and rope, but still.

You say, "Can I ask you something?"

I say, "Always."

You say, "You don't have to . . . but I have an idea . . ."

I'm nervous. I imagine all the things
you could say.

You say, "I think that's what we should do."

"What?" I ask
but I already know.

We stare at each other.

I say, "Aaron?"

You say, "Oliver?"

I'm touching your face
and you're touching mine.

I imagine us as
the soldiers' bodies.

It's kind of sad, maybe,
even scary, I guess, but not
in the moment.

Scary because deciding who you are
feels so much more permanent
than anything else we've ever done.

Maybe we are their bodies
here in the attic of an old farmhouse
in Pennsylvania.

"I'm Oliver," I say to you, crying.

And you say, "I'm Aaron."

ON A NIGHT IN 1778

I tell you that tonight
we should pretend to be the soldiers.

You laugh and say I'm ridiculous
but you play along
and crawl into the bottom bunk.

We're silent for a few moments,
both of us getting into character.

I realize I don't really know
what people talked like back then.
I can think of Shakespeare's plays

with the *thee* and *thou*
and I can think of the language
of the Declaration of Independence . . .
but how did they sound when they made jokes?

How can we know
without hearing their voices?

They must have had words for *queer*—
maybe subtle ways to hint
at where their genders or sexualities
bloomed away from the norm.

You whisper, "Hello? Friend?
Are you awake?"

I smile. "Yes, brother,
I am."

"Are the others asleep?"
you ask.

I peer over the side of my bunk.
"I think they are."

You crawl up into bed with me.
You say, "I have thought about you
all day and night for weeks."

I say, "Stay here with me.
No one will notice."

Then we laugh and a part of me
wishes we'd kept pretending longer
and another part of me thinks
I'm too old to pretend.

WHILE I'M ASLEEP YOU LEAVE
ME TEXT MESSAGES

You're always teasing me
about how I can't help but fall asleep first.

About a month ago
you started doing this thing
where you'd text me while I was asleep,
so when I wake up
I always check my phone right away.

You text:

> Hey there
> You're snoring but it's cute.
>
> Are you having a dream?
>
> I hope you're dreaming about being in 1778
> Haha that's your fantasy right?
>
> Oliver Oliver
>
> I can't sleep but I don't want to wake you up
>
> I'm worried about the future
>
> How did we get to be in high school?
>
> We were just like awkward sixth graders last week
>
> See you in the morning!

And I want to pick up the conversation
but now you're still asleep
so instead I lie back down
and close my eyes a little longer.

BREAKFAST

After sleepovers Mom
always makes pancakes for us.

She's been doing it since
grade school back when I
had other kids and not just you over.

The smell would creep through the house
and up to my bedroom,
filling the walls with sweet vanilla
and syrup smell.

We get up and
there's no pancake smell this time.

You're still asleep so
I go downstairs in my pajamas
to the kitchen lit by
the amber-gray glow of morning.

Mom's set out the pancake mix
on the counter with
a note that reads

Give it a try this time!
and a little heart drawn next to it.

While the note doesn't say it,

I know this means that
Mom knows me and
you are together.

She might not say it for a while
but I know Mom.

She drops hints like this,
circling close enough
to the truth until I
break down and tell her everything.

I read the instructions
and you come down
and hug me from behind.
I pretend that this is our house
and we're grown up
and we have a dog and
we're home for the day
on the weekend with each other.

You kiss my neck
and I want you to push
me up against the wall
in the kitchen.

I want you more
each day and this morning
it's almost unbearable.

I want you to take off
my clothes here in
the kitchen,

ridiculous like in TV
when people have spontaneous
sex on countertops.

I'm embarrassed that I
think about this while
trying to read the instructions on
the back of the pancake box.

You step to
the side and sigh as you read Mom's note,

saying, "Your Mom knows,
doesn't she?"

BLUEBERRIES

You go digging in the freezer
and find a bag of frozen blueberries

all the way in the back
and pour them right into the batter.

I wonder for a second
what kind of food the soldiers Aaron and Oliver
would have eaten
on a morning after sleeping next to each other.

You say, "You can't call
me Aaron in front of my parents."

"Okay," I say even though
it hurts.

"And I won't be able to
call you Oliver."

I nod, stirring. That hurts too.

I wish that we lived
in a different world.

"My parents aren't bad," you say.

"I know."

"My parents love me."

"I know they do."

"They're just really busy right now."

The first pancake sizzles
as I pour batter
in the greased cast-iron pan.

I get the spatula ready.

"You mean busy with José."

You don't cry often.
I have only seen
you cry once

but you start crying.

The pan is spitting
so I turn down the heat and hug you.

"What's happening? Did I say something?"

You sit down at the breakfast table
and tuck your knees into
your chest.

"I was going to tell you earlier," you say.

The pan hissing.

"About what? You can tell me anything."

"It's hard," you say.

The batter crackling, louder than it should, louder
than when Mom makes them.

"Try, it's okay. You can tell me."

You look at me
and bury your head
in my chest.

I pet your hair with my one free hand,
spatula in the other.

"My family is moving
in two weeks."

The words' meaning doesn't register.

THE SOLTEROS

have always lived here.

As long as I've known
the street names
they've lived

in their big house out
at the edge of town

with the tall windows on the first floor
like wide eyes open.

Mr. Soltero loves antiques so
he scours the market to find
paintings and sketches of the house from the 1800s.

He loves the house. Sometimes when
I've been over, he's pulled us aside
to show us some small detail
like the gutters he put on himself
or the new umbrella on the deck.

At night when I've walked past, I have
looked in those big windows
and seen all of you in the living room.

I've turned back to take in the big, beautiful house
many times before walking to

Mom's blue station wagon parked at the end
of the driveway to pick me up.

You, Aaron, watch TV together with them each night
and Mrs. Soltero
makes delicious food

that fills the whole world with wonderful smells.

While the sun still sets late you and I know
when to come by the smell billowing from
the house.

My parents don't cook much
unless it's a holiday, so I'm always excited
to eat with your family.

My favorite is tostones, which kind of taste like potato latkes
but better.

Your mom only makes those on weekends when
she's not coming back late from work
at the old-people home.

Your family is warm and

you're all involved at Holy Guardian Angels.

Your parents are in the parents' club at school.

I hold on to your shirt.

Why can't you just stay to finish
senior year?

Then we'll be free and
your family can move wherever.

"No, why? Why can't you stay?"

AARON, WHY CAN'T YOU STAY?

You say,

> "I can't talk about it,
> it's too much to talk about now
> when my mom is going to pick me up
> in an hour.
>
> I will explain.
> It's not fair, any of it.
> I hate how fast everything is happening.
>
> It's just too much.
>
> I can't stay longer.
> I have to go.
>
> I swear it's not you but
> can I just have a sec?"

You go upstairs.

PANCAKES

The first pancake was terribly burned
and all the blueberries turned black
at the bottom of the pan.

I wash out the pan and start again,
putting a little drop of margarine
on the pan bottom and swirling it around
till all the edges are covered.

I hear you move upstairs.

I imagine you undressing
in front of the full-length mirror
that hangs on my door.

The pancake bubbles but this
time I flip it over when it's golden brown—
as perfect as

your bare skin,
doubled in the reflection.

I hear you walk to the other
end of my bedroom.

The floorboards creak.

I want the pancake to be perfect for you
so that it might make you want to
call your parents to stay longer.

TIME MACHINE

I am imagining a time machine
we could escape through.

We could just go and live
as those soldiers.

We wouldn't have to worry
about college. We could move somewhere new

where no one knew our old selves.
You text me,

I'm sorry I'm taking so long.
I meant to tell you earlier . . .
I just. I just was enjoying everything so much.
I didn't want to ruin it.

I pretend the text is from
a carrier pigeon. I want to write back
and tell you my plan
to escape to 1778 but I know
it's not helpful—I know it's not real.

MORE PANCAKES

I make the whole bowl of batter
and you still haven't come down.

I stack the pancakes up nice
on two plates

one for you and one for me.

My parents must be avoiding
running into us.

They've always been awkward
around my friends; I can't
imagine how they'd be around a boyfriend.

Oliver and Aaron
are all I think about

How they went to war together
and how they had to also bear
the secret that they were trans
without even having the language to
explain it.

I wonder what the real Oliver would do
if he learned Aaron was leaving?

Maybe they had to join
different regiments—maybe they parted ways
and remembered Valley Forge
as their home, carrying it with them
as the war continued.

Who told who when they had to leave?

Were they eating?

Did Oliver think of running away
from the war,

from their lives forever?

Because that's all
I can think about.

COLD PANCAKES

The pancakes are kinda
gross by the time you get down.

I thought I'd be cute and drizzle the syrup
on in little patterns but then
they just got all soggy.

You sit down next to me.

Your eyes are red.
I know you were crying.

I could hear you
but you've told me before
you like to be alone when you cry.

You eat the pancakes even
though they have to be a mess by now.

I don't touch mine.
I'm too upset to feel like eating.

"You know I still care about you
and I want to be with you," you say.

I nod. I don't want to show
how upset I am.
I want
to focus on you.

Cutting the pancakes with
the side of my fork, I pretend I'm eating.

You set the fork down.

"You promise not to tell anyone?"

"Of course," I say, even though
I'm not sure about what.

About the soldiers? About us?
About you leaving?

JOSÉ

It's hard for you, Aaron, to tell me about José.

You don't know where to start so
you start off by just talking about him.

He's your brother.

Two years older.

He doesn't talk much
when I'm over but he always
says a gentle "hello."

You, Aaron, say,

"José, he serves every mass
that he can at church.

He comes in Saturdays
and Sundays.

José loves God. I always wish
I loved God like José does.

He was always so sure about
being a priest.

I was always thankful for that because
it meant that no one would
expect me to be a nun or anything.

My parents love José.
He's amazing. The best son, they always say.

He's always been so nice to me.

I told José I was gay and he still loved me.
He sticks up for queer people at church
even when it means other
people will think he's gay.

José saw something at church
and he had to tell someone."

I don't understand so I just stare at you and nod.

"José's why we have to move,
because something happened.
I'm sorry.
I should have
told you in a better way.
This is a mess."

I still don't understand
but I pretend that I do.

I think about José and again about how I wish I had
a brother like him.

I hope he's all right.

UPS AND DOWNS

Your mom picks you up
and you don't hug me goodbye.

You finished your pancakes,
not talking.

I tried to understand what you meant when
you talked about José.

I felt stupid for not knowing
and there I was sitting with you
and not asking you more questions.

I wave to you as your clanky tan car
drives off and I feel like
you're leaving and I'll never see
you again.

Inside I clean dishes.

Mom and Dad come down
and none of us talk.

I hate it.

No one talking.

But then the doorbell rings.

I go to get it and it's a package
for you!

Your chest binder.

I'm excited about it.

I sign for it without even thinking
that my parents are right across
the room.

All I can think about
is helping you put it on.

It's strange, all these emotions in a day.
I close the front door,
package in hand.

"What's that?" Mom asks.

WHAT'S THAT?

I open your package in front of her.

It's perfect, a gc2b nude No. 2,
beige like your skin. I always think of binders
as like a part of a trans person's body.

I hold up the binder and explain,
"This is a chest binder,
it flattens your chest,

it helps trans people express their gender."

I'm nervous while I talk,
scared to show how much I
have read about this.

Dad nods and just says,
"That's interesting."

Mom asks, "Why that . . . color?"

"Oh, it's for . . ."

And I realize they don't know
your name yet. I'm not sure

what to call you.

I'm not sure if you'd want
my parents to know.

I imagine your old name
fluttering in a jar, trapped.

I say, "They . . . my friend . . . [****].
They don't go by that name anymore
but I feel I want to ask them
before I tell you more."

"We won't tell anyone," Mom says.

"I know, but like for privacy."

Mom sighs.

Dad asks, "Do you want one of those?"

Without thinking I respond, "Yes, yes I do."

"We can order one."

Mom asks, "Is it safe? That seems like it could hurt your chest."

"I'll send you some links to articles about binding.
It's okay if you're careful."

I never imagined it like this.

I'm nervous but
the conversation moves easily.

No one is upset.

I knew my parents loved me but
I always wondered if this
would change that

and now I know it won't.

I feel so lucky
and then so sad that it's
not like this for everyone.

I WANT TO KEEP YOU SAFE

"Will you not tell his parents . . . please," I say.

Mom surveys the binder I'm holding.

"We can't lie . . . you have to know that.
We would be so hurt if someone
didn't keep us in the loop about you . . .
But I won't say anything directly,
only if they ask."

This makes me furious at Mom but
I understand. I wish she knew

the kinds of things that can happen
to trans people.
I just want everything to be okay for you.

THEY KNOW . . .

"Another thing," Mom says.

She looks at the floor, so I know what's coming.

"No more sleepovers . . . for now, until we talk."

"I kind of knew you were going to say that."

"We don't care who you love, but we wouldn't let
you have a sleepover with . . . a boy. So we can't
just let you have a sleepover with . . . [****]."

"What if they are a boy?"

"Well . . . you know what I mean," Mom says.

"We have to talk about you having sleepovers
with boyfriends or girlfriends or . . . just . . . friends."

I'm frustrated at first but
I feel good because this means that

they see us.

THE BINDER

I set your binder on
the top of my dresser still in the wrapping.

The rest of the day
I return to look at it.

Mom says we're going to pick one out tonight
(after she reads the article I sent her about binding . . . ugh).

I know I should tell you right away.

I know you'll be happy
to know it came and you'll get
to wear it soon

and yet I want to have some
time alone with it.

I know I shouldn't but
I want to try it on.

I type: hey im sorry if this morning was weird.
ur wonderful. i have some happy news . . .

YOUR BINDER IS HERE!

But I don't send it.

I put the phone down on my nightstand.

I slide your binder out
of the glossy packaging.

The material is swishy
and smooth,

almost futuristic.

At first it seems like it might not fit,
like I might get trapped in it if I tried.

I wish you were here to help me.

That thought makes me sad because
I should be helping you put on the binder.

I manage to get it over my head
and wiggle till it sits just right,

binding my chest.

Looking in the mirror
I move my hands across the fabric
covering my chest.

So nice and flat.

It's how I've been wanting to look.

I pose at all angles.

I don't let myself take a picture because
that feels like betrayal

but I love it.

The binder isn't comfortable
but it makes me want

to run outside and walk
into town

to show it off.

TRAPPED

I can't
get the
binder off
any way
I wriggle.

This is
the first time
I think about
God for
a long time.

I don't
know if
I believe
in God

but my
first thought
is that
he might
be punishing me
for using
your binder.

Then I think,
That's stupid.
Why would
God know
this is happening?

I smile,
imagining God
as a trans person,
maybe nonbinary
or gender-fluid.

Maybe when
God comes
they'll be
a queer person.
I wish I had someone
to share this idea with.

Maybe they
oscillate between
different genders
each day.

I have
friends I've
met on Tumblr
who are
like that,

their genders
flowing like
the creek
by your house.

I wish
I knew more
people
like us

in real
life.

I'm scared
to come out
at school
without you

and being
trapped in
the binder
makes it feel
like I'm
suffocating.

Mom
hears me
crying.

She opens
the door
and helps
me take
the binder
off.

She holds
me and says
that we'll
find one

that fits me.

LEAVING I

There have been times where
two weeks has felt like
forever.

When I was younger every summer
I'd get to pick a camp.

So much happened in those two weeks.

In middle school they were all
sleepaway camps.

The last year I went was in eighth grade
and I tried a computer-programming camp.

It was all boys besides me
and this girl Ellen.

Ellen had a pixie cut
and she wore the same
rose flower crown every day.

I never paid attention to the camp activities
so I learned literally nothing about programming

but I did learn a lot about Ellen.

At lunch I sat with her
at a picnic table.

She ate blackberries and
peanut butter and honey sandwiches

every day.

We talked more and more
and the last day she
kissed me in the bathroom.

It felt like I had known Ellen
forever.

Like I had lived a whole
lifetime in those two weeks.

I feel like everything is going
to blur past

in these last two weeks
you live in your house
at the edge of town.

LEAVING II

We go through our normal routines.

We don't talk about
you moving.

Sometimes I even forget
anything is going to change.

On either rusted rail
of the train tracks that run
in the field by my house
we walk and list all the movies
that we want to watch together someday.

I say *Juno* and
Nick & Norah's Infinite Playlist.

You say
Pulp Fiction and
Corpse Bride.

And then you admit that you
haven't even seen *Pulp Fiction,*
that you just think it sounds cool.

LEAVING III

We live as if we were going
to graduate together in June,

both of us side by side in navy blue
caps and gowns.

One afternoon you say,
"It'll be over soon, our senior year,"

and I'm not sure if you remember we're
not going to spend the rest of it together.

I don't want to remind you
but tears gather in the corners of my eyes.

I wipe them on the backs of my hands
and you ask, "What, what did I say?"

LEAVING IV

I help you put on the binder
and you laugh when I
tell you that I broke
it in for you.

You make me try it on
and I flex in the mirror.

You put your hand on
my flattened chest
and it feels right,

and I think of kissing you,
both of us wearing binders.

LEAVING V

The leaves have started to turn,
so we've collected them in piles
in your backyard.

I burrow under.

We have never jumped in leaf piles
like normal kids.
We have always used them
like little forts.

When we were little, we'd
be rabbits or bears
under those layers
of damp orange and red.

LEAVING VI

Sometimes you start
to cry and I never know what
of the thousand things it could be
that's causing it.

Are you going to miss me?

Are you upset about
not being able to
tell your parents you're Aaron
not [****]?

Are you upset about
whatever happened with José?

I don't ask.
I just want to enjoy the time with you.

LEAVING VII

You are there when I
tell my parents my name,

after school on Friday
when you come over for dinner.

"I'm using the name Oliver," I say.

And you tell them
you use the name Aaron.

And we both tell the story
of the soldiers.

Mom and Dad don't seem to understand
why we care so much about the soldiers.

It's true we have no proof they were real,
but the Twitter thread is enough for us.

Mom gets out her phone at the table
and shows me a book
about "gay America"
she saw online.

She says, "It reminded me
of you."

And I know
she's listening.

LEAVING VIII

There's too much happening
right now.

Your family moves
on Sunday

and the night before
I don't get to see you.

I pace my house, alternating
between looking at my phone
and hoping you'll text me

and rereading chapters of
my latest history book.

We're onto the Second World War
in class and I wonder

what history class will be like
at your new school.

It's nearly ten at night
when you text me:

i have an idea!

AN IDEA

You (Aaron): wat if we wrote to each other . . .
like of course we can still text and stuff but wat if we wrote?

Me (Oliver): how? like letters?

You (Aaron): letters like the two soldiers would have.

Me (Oliver): Yes! Each week!!!

You (Aaron): I promise, I will. That'll be great!

Me (Oliver): Me too, I love that.

You (Aaron): Let's just write letters. No texting
It'll be romantic!

Me (Oliver): Oh wow, that would be interesting

You (Aaron): Like distant lovers!

Me (Oliver): Yeah.

You (Aaron): I want to go to my new school with my new name.

Me (Oliver): Aw, that would be great! I'm here for you.

You (Aaron): I know you are but you also . . .
aren't. I mean you are but not in person.

Me (Oliver): You can text me!

You (Aaron): Mhm

Me (Oliver): You'll send me your new address?

You (Aaron): Yes!

Me (Oliver): Hey, I'm sorry that I'm telling you this over a text message but I love you and I'm sorry we didn't do anything special this week.

You (Aaron): I'm glad we didn't. It made it less weird. Did your parents ask?

Me (Oliver): I told them you're moving.

You (Aaron): Do they know why?

Me (Oliver): I don't even know why.

You (Aaron): It's hard to explain, we'll talk more though

Me (Oliver): I love you

You (Aaron): I don't know if I want to say that yet. Like not over text messages. It's too much right now there's just all this shit happening I want to say it right.

Me (Oliver): I understand that! I'm sorry if you felt like I wanted to make you do something.

You (Aaron): No! It's okay.

Me (Oliver): You'll text me your drawings?

You (Aaron): Yep!

Me (Oliver): Safe travels tomorrow

IT'S HARD TO EXPLAIN

I don't believe
in coincidences.

Nope.

The day you leave is the same
day that the story is in the paper.

Mom reads the paper
and hands Dad the comics section
as usual.

I see the headline

"Priest Child Abuse: Hundreds of Possible Victims"

I slide the chair closer
to read more

but I stop when I see
the name of your church.

Holy Guardian Angels.

"Mom, did you read that story?" I ask.

Mom nods. She breathes deep
and her grip on the edges

of the paper tightens.

"Yes, I did, it's very, very sad."

"That's where the Solteros go. Went."

"Yes," Mom says.

Dad looks up from the comics page
and half closes the paper.

They both look at me.

They name
your brother later in the article.

José Soltero

was the first to come forward
to the police.

I don't want to tell
you that I know all of this,

it all seems too personal
for me to know,

for everyone reading
the *Morning Call* to know.

I want to hold you.

I want to take the fifteen-minute walk to your house.

I want to text you more and

I want to text you every morning
of every day.

I feel terrible for it.

I don't want to make things harder for
you.

After all, I'm not the one moving.

I want to take the fifteen-minute walk to your house.

I want the creek.

I want the smell of dinner coaxing us inside.

But you're unpacking.

You're in Queens,

New York, where your uncle and aunt live.

I googled it and there's a bus
on the other side of town

that makes trips to the city.

Three hours or so

isn't too far, is it?

I decide I'll save up money to get the bus,

but until then,

I'll write
I'll write
I'll write
I'll write
I'll write
I'll write
I'll write
I'll write
I'll write
I'll write
I'll write
I'll write
I'll write
I'll write
I'll write
I'll write
I'll write
I'll write
I'll write
I'll write
I'll write
I'll write
I'll write
I'll write
I'll write

I'll write
I'll write
I'll write
I'll write
I'll write

II
LETTERS

THE WAR

Dear Aaron, I write

Did I ever tell you about

how in the Revolution they fought
most battles
just standing in rows?

One side

                          facing

the other

                        across

a field.

Two parallel lines.

Dad says that's why
the Revolutionary War
is so boring, because
there were so many
customs around how battles
were supposed to be carried out.

Did you know sometimes
there were even spectators?

I remind myself
on the worst days
that there were those soldiers,

younger than us,

who had to stand and face boys
just as young as them—
who had to aim faulty muskets
and hope the odds landed in their favor.

The truth is, Aaron,
I like reading about war
because I
can focus

on the machinery and the uniforms
and distract myself

from all the dying.

My parents are worried
about me coming out.

Mom says I should just wait

till college.

I know they care but

every time someone calls me

[****]

I feel like I'm standing on one side
of a battlefield by myself.

I want to say, "Oliver, Oliver.
Please just call me Oliver."

But it's hard to correct people.

I know if you were here
you'd stand up for me.

I'm sorry this letter is all about me.

Tell me about you.

—Oliver

    It's thrilling
to get to write my name down.

    I feel more real
each time I write it.

THE WAR

You write,

            Dear Oliver,

        My new school isn't bad really.

           I just feel alone.

      The people at school aren't even bad.

    In fact, for the first time in forever
    I'm not in a sea of white people.

        But I still feel different.

         I don't know anyone
       or where people hang out
         or what is cool
        or where I fit in.

    You know, I always thought of cities as
       super loud all the time
    but really their noise is just different.

    Nights in Kutztown are full of birdcalls
    and insect songs and revving engines
    and people blasting bad country music.

I miss my window
that looked out into the woods.

But sometimes I'm grateful
for the three horn sounds
as the LIRR train rolls out of Jamaica Station or
the sound of someone singing loudly
in their apartment nearby.

Listening to the sounds at night
makes me feel lonely, too.
Like everyone else
has lives here.
Everyone but me.

It's so stupid for me to feel alone
because everyone fucking feels alone.
It's just hard. I just
feel mechanical.

I never knew that that was why
you like war stuff,
about being able to focus
on the machines instead
of dying.

That makes sense.

I think you like
learning about war
for the same reason

I like superheroes
and comic books.

They help distract
from everything.

I don't think my parents
get it.

I did actually
tell them . . .
well I wrote them a letter
and slipped it
under their door.

I basically just said
"I'm a boy now,
okay?"

They didn't change pronouns
or anything.

Maybe they can't understand.
Maybe they think it's a phase.

When I sit down at the dinner table
Mom emphasizes things she didn't before.

This week she said, "I saw a dress
in the thrift shop
you'd look perfect in"

and

"Have any boys asked you
to the winter formal dance?"

and

"Mija, you should let
tu prima
teach you how to
do your makeup nice
for college interviews."

Dad just doesn't say anything.

At dinner he looks past me.
When I come sit in the living room
sometimes he'll even leave
and go up to his room
to be alone.

I almost wish they'd
be mad at me,
maybe that'd be easier to
deal with.

I know I should
try to tell José.

I feel like he might understand.
Maybe he could help
my parents understand.

I haven't told him.

Should I?

I know this sounds dramatic
but I don't know if I will
ever tell him.

At school I told the art teacher,
Ms. Soto,
and she lets me sit with her during lunch
to work on my drawings.

I guess she's my one friend.
That's pretty sad but it
could be worse,
right?

It's only
part of a year, so it's okay if I don't
talk to anyone here, right?

I've been thinking about college.

I should think about college, right?

Everything's just changed so much
so fucking fast.

Do you think about
like hormones and stuff?

When I'm eighteen I'm going
to get into the clinic and get them.

I turn eighteen in like . . . what?
Three months!

Do you want hormones?

You don't have to want them,
I know not everyone does.

I keep thinking that like maybe
if I take testosterone maybe
people will start to like "see me,"

you know?

I don't know. You should visit.

My parents are too busy with José to
give a fuck what I do anymore.

(I mean they don't do anything about
José, they just loom over him
and pray by themselves and shit.)

Remember how they always like
make me text them a million times
when I go anywhere?

They don't anymore.

I know I hated it but it makes me sad
that they don't even care now.

I feel like I don't exist.

I know these are two totally different things
but why do they believe José
but not me?

José doesn't talk to me much,
at least not like he used to.

I can't talk to him about
being trans.
I know he's dealing with other stuff.

—Aaron

UNIFORMS I

Dear Aaron, I write,

It's hard to only
write to you.

I want to hear
your voice.

I want to call you on the phone but I know
you're busy or maybe
you're not busy
but busy in the sense
that you need space.

My mom was really nice to
me today.

We argued again about
me coming out to the school.

I told her I was going to do it
even if she didn't want me to.

She cried and said she just wanted me
to be safe.

Later she said
she had to go to the mall to return some
work clothes.

I went along and
she took me shopping
in the boys' section.

Through the boys' dressing room door
we talked.

We talked about hormones
and all those things.

She cried again which made
me annoyed because it's not like
she has to really go through anything.

But at least she cares.

I don't think I want hormones, though.

I just want people to see me.

If everyone could see me
how you do

everything

would be

okay.

—Oliver

BEAUTIFUL OR WHATEVER

You (Aaron): i wanted to keep things like casual
or whatever by not texting you and just seeing how
the letters go but i had to tell you that i sent my first
portfolio to some art schools!!!! im super nervous
but im going to email it to you. Right now
I just sent it to NYU, Pratt, and the New School . . .
shooting high . . . or is it aiming high?

You (Aaron): im sorry if that ruins
the magic of the letters. i just
wanted to tell you.

You (Aaron): r u okay? r u mad?

Me (Oliver): that's amazing! sorry i put my phone down
i don't check it as much as i used to. ha. i only
text you so lol why check it.

You (Aaron): aw

Me (Oliver): im so happy for you.

UNIFORMS II

Dear Aaron, I write again,
and I feel like I must be bothering you

I know sometimes
it's hard to write.

It's okay if you don't write
every week.

I'm not upset that you missed one week,
I just want to know you're okay
there in New York.

Tell me about what else is different.
Are there lots of queer people there?
Artists? Musicians? I can't imagine.
Haha, probably less cows.

I'm okay here
in Kutztown.

I mean what I said though
about the French uniforms
(did you know there
were French soldiers
in the American Revolution?).

My dad says they're impractical
but I started talking to him

about doing reenacting maybe
on the weekends.

He's been trying to make
me get a "hobby"

plus, I've had two years
of French in school so might as well
put it to work.

I'm going to wear part of the uniform
for Halloween
because I didn't have time

to pull anything else together.

I don't have anyone to go with
but I didn't want to tell my parents that.

I want to text you so often . . .

Write to me when you have time

if you have time

take your time.

Love,

Oliver

NOVEMBER I

You, Aaron, write,

Sometimes I think about

how much time I wasted being
a girl.

It fucking sucks.

You know if we were really our soldiers
we wouldn't have been able to know
that we were men and we wouldn't
have known each other. We wouldn't
have had the language to describe
what it means to be
two gay trans men—I think about

that sometimes. How it's a coincidence
that I was born in this time and you were
born in this time.
I want to be straight up with you, Oliver,
it's hard for me

to write to you.

I feel like there's a lot you don't/can't
understand. Your family is so nice,
I wish you guys could just keep me,
but at the same time
I love my family.

I know I love my family but I wish it was easier.
I can't imagine a life without my family.

For so long our house in town
was like an escape
from the town all around me
who saw me as different
for being Puerto Rican.

In our walls we spoke Spanglish
without hesitation. We laughed and
ate and watched TV and played board games
and sometimes we prayed.

Even though the city is so different from Kutztown,
in some ways it feels the same.
It feels lonely and huge.
A giant maze.

On the first day of school
a woman at the office
handed me my schedule
without saying anything else.

I had no idea
how the rooms were even numbered.

So I wandered around.

There were police at like
every single corner
and I felt like they were watching me,
waiting for me to mess up.

I was so afraid of getting in trouble
or of them thinking I was trying
to skip my classes.

I was just lost.

I passed the art room
and I walked inside like I belonged there.

Students were quietly working on projects.

I rushed over to the teacher.
I was so scrambled.

I just asked,
"Hi, I'm so sorry. I'm just really lost
and I'm an artist and I thought
it might be good to ask for help here."

Ms. Soto. Thank God for her, seriously.
The class was just working
on their paintings
so she brought me up to her desk.
She let me show her my schedule
and then later, during her free period,
she showed me to each of the classrooms.

The art room was always a second home
in Kutztown, but now it feels
like my only home.

My real house doesn't feel
like an escape.

It's full of my parents' worries
about José and me.
I know it takes time but
I've waited so long to be myself.

I don't want to be a downer.

I did make a friend at school, though
(besides the art teacher—ha!)

Their name is Ryan.
I noticed their nonbinary flag
pinned to their backpack
and I was like "I have to introduce myself."

It took me like way too long
to just walk over and say
"Hi there, I'm Aaron.
I like your flag."

I'm really thankful
for that pin—
for the symbols we have
to show other queer people
where we are.

They draw too
and we're thinking of writing
a comic together.

You would like them!

I think about you all the time, though,
I do.

I wish I could explain how
I simultaneously can't talk
to you and miss you.

—Aaron

EQUIVALENT TO DEATH

Dear Aaron, I write

Today we had our first snow day
and I spent it watching the snowflakes
swell larger and larger,
collecting on roofs and across town.

It's strange to think
not so long ago we shared the last heat of summer
walking in the woods and across the creek.

All day I've been reading online
about the American Revolution.

Two things I discovered:
1) Puerto Rican AND Jewish people fought in it!
There are people online with the same question we have—
why don't we hear about people like us?
There are documents and photographs
and letters and so much more!
I hope someday
I can be someone who discovers these things
for other people to find
on snow days.

2) There's real writing by a trans man soldier!!!
His name was Robert Shurtleff
and he even took on "male" roles on his farm
before the war. How did he make sense
of himself in a world without the language
to explain he didn't feel like the gender
he was told he should be?

When he was wounded in battle, he wrote,
"I considered this as a death wound,
or as being the equivalent of it,
as it must, I thought,
lead to the discovery of my sex."
How horrible to constantly feel scared of being discovered
in the midst of battles and war
and disease and hunger.
People like us have always been so brave.

Please don't think this is too cheesy but
I think you are so brave and we
are going to be okay.

All day I've been thinking about
how if you still lived a few blocks away
I might be able
to put on my snow boots
and trudge to visit you,
leaving a trail of footprints behind.

Love you,

Oliver

NOVEMBER II

Dear Aaron, I write

Usually at this time in November
we would be enjoying how
easy it is to explore

the woods when the brush
and weeds
start to die.

The grass turns brown and crunchy
in November.

I've been thinking about the forest
and how some of the trees are so old
they might have been around
during the Revolution.

I imagine our soldiers
walking in the woods together
away from town
to avoid anyone seeing them.

Maybe if someone did pass by
they might say
"We're hunting" or "We're fishing."

Then they'd walk away
and kiss behind
a giant fallen tree. They'd smell

the same wet leaves and soil
we smelled when we followed one another
between sturdy maple trees,
twigs snapping beneath our feet.

That would be
what our soldiers smelled
as they made their own secret path
through the woods.

I wish I knew why you didn't
want to talk or text.

I'm not upset.
I just wish
I had someone.

My first reenacting event my dad
is going to go with me

which will be interesting because
my dad and I hardly ever talk (you know that).

Are we still dating?

I know that's stupid to ask
but I'm worried you don't want to be.

It would be okay if you didn't
want to be.

I just don't know how to understand things.

I should finish my college applications.
The deadlines are coming up.

Mom wants me to apply to
six colleges.

I picked them all in the city,
near you.

She made me pick at
least three that are

far away.

I would go for history,

but you know that already.

Speaking of which!

In class we'll start covering

the 1950s and '60s soon.

Time is moving so fast.

Greg Ollen asked if I wanted

to play Call of Duty.

*It was funny, I bet they just needed
someone else since you're gone.*

*Greg and I have only ever
talked about homework before
he asked.*

Maybe you would be proud of me.

*I agreed even though
you know how I feel about being
distracted in class.*

*It turns out I'm better at multitasking
than I thought. Though, to be fair,*

*I really really really suck
at* Call of Duty.

Maybe you can give me some tips . . .

*Also, I feel bad
that things have been so hard for you*

and not so bad for me.

I wish I could take some of that weight off.

*I feel bad when I tell you the good things
that happen.*

I know you don't want to right now

but if you want to call

please call me

or text me or

send me some comics!

Love,

Oliver

And this time
when I write my name
it starts to feel natural,
like it was there
all along.

COMIC PANELS I

From you, Aaron:

[Image of a boy in a big hoodie.
The boy is holding a balloon and
walking down the city street.
The sky in the background is orange
and rose. The buildings are all black.
The balloon is blue.]

[Image of a boy in a big hoodie.
The boy is tying his balloon
to his backpack.]

[Image of a boy in a big hoodie.
The balloon is lifting the boy so
that he can see the whole city.]

[Image of the whole city.
The buildings are still black,
just silhouettes.]

[Image of the boy's face.
Pale like Oliver's face.
Blue eyes reflecting orange
and pink from the sunset.]

[Image of a different boy.
This boy has a paintbrush
and a palette.]

[Image of a different boy.
He's walked to the edge of the city,
right up to the sky. He's painting the sky.
The sky is his painting: watercolor.
The colors drip together.]

BOY IN A BIG HOODIE

Me (Oliver): i love your drawings.

Me (Oliver): i love how you don't use words
to describe things
how the images you make capture the kinds
of emotions and thoughts
that there are no words for.

Me (Oliver): Am i the boy in the big hoodie?

Me (Oliver): You don't have to tell me anytime soon
but are you the boy painting?

Me (Oliver): i wear that big hoodie all the time now.
partially because it's freezing and partially
because i like how it hides my body.

Me (Oliver): i wear the big hoodie on days when
i don't feel like putting on a binder

Me (Oliver): im sorry i text you so much.
don't feel like you need to respond.
i just didn't want to wait till
the letter to tell you about the pictures.

REENACTING

Dear Aaron, I write

*I'm writing to you from
the ACTUAL war front today.*

*I don't like reenacting like I thought I would
so I'm hiding in a bush.*

*I mean, I liked the dressing up but
I don't like how loud*

the cannons are.

Each explosion pounds against my whole body.

*I started shaking, it began
in my knees.*

I don't like seeing walls of soldiers
falling in the rows,
and the smoke rising in
the wake of the charge.

Dad is way too into it.

He shouts and raises his bayonet
at the other side.

Last night around the fire
I realized I'm the youngest
person here,

which is strange because
in the real war there would
have been so many more boys my age.

All the men assume
I'm my dad's son.

Dad almost corrected them
until he realized they were right.

It's exciting to be gendered
correctly but I'm not sure
if I want to go to war again like this.

I feel like I'm being disrespectful
to people who really died in the Revolution,

like our soldiers.

How do you think
you would feel if people
were reenacting our lives

sometime in the distant future?

Strange, right?

I don't know,

something to think about.

Love,

Oliver

THANKSGIVING

Dear Aaron, I write again
      and I wonder if you
      are reading my letters
      but I decide I have to trust you.

If they really were lovers,

our two soldiers,

how do you think they did it?

How did they stay
connected?

How could they stand
not knowing anything about
the other
if they traveled apart?

Maybe they spent
years apart, living with the dream
they might see each other again.

It makes me feel like I'm dramatic

for being so upset at not
talking for a month or so.

Forget I asked about dating.

I don't even care about that.
I just
care about you.

How are you?

How is your family?

I applied to three colleges,
three more to go.

It's not important where.
As long as it's in the city,
I just kind of let the school counselor
tell me where I'll probably get in.

History excites me but
I can't get excited about college.

My parents have me going to a therapist now too.

It's kind of surreal. They have
a leather couch like therapists in
cartoons. The couch alone

made me want to cry.

I can't tell if it makes things better
or worse to talk about.

I started telling people
to call me Oliver.

In gym class I'm still in the girls' class
and so the gym teacher

still calls me [****].

I hate how sad it makes me.

I don't hate who I was
I just
want people to see me how I am,

for who I am.

I told her I go by Oliver but
I don't think she understands what
that means.

I wish I could talk to you
in the woods behind your
house or in the bunk bed
upstairs.

I want to kiss you.

I've been thinking about
that a lot.

Also I started eating lunch with Greg
and the other guys from history class.

It was strange at first.

I'm scared of high school boys,
which is funny
because I am one.

You remember Greg's friend
Callen? He said this awful thing
about never wanting to go down
on his girlfriend
casually while
eating a bologna sandwich.

He was talking about how
horrifying vaginas are and I know

trans guys don't usually like
their vagina but I don't mind mine
and it pissed me off that he
was just talking about this girl's
vagina to us.

She can do better.

Maybe all straight girls can do better.

Of course, I didn't say that.

I just kind of nodded and then I
was like "maybe you should talk
about it to her."

I kept wondering
what you would have said
if you were there.

I feel like you would have
made a joke or something
to let Callen know he's kind of
an asshole.

This is becoming a long letter.

I started off thinking
I was going to tell you that it'll
be Thanksgiving in . . . two days

and I'm going to miss
meeting up with you on that
Friday like we used to.

I might come out to my whole extended family.

I'm scared.

We'll see.

I hope you enjoy it, the long letter I mean.

I hope you're doing okay.

I love you.

Should I stop saying that?

—Oliver

TIPS FOR *CALL OF DUTY*

Oh, Oliver,
you write

If I was there, I'd give you a real
CoD crash course . . . most of the stuff
I'd kind of have to show you.

We had a shitty Thanksgiving.

Mom misses Kutztown.

Dad says he doesn't
but he does.

There's nowhere quite like it
to satisfy his antiquing cravings—haha.

It's funny how in a city with SO MUCH
we are missing these tiny stupid things
from Kutztown. It's ridiculous!

And honestly sometimes
I can't even enjoy the cool things in the city
like the museum or the sculptures at the park
because I'm always like
"Man, I want to show Oliver that."

Mom sometimes wishes that José
would have handled everything different,
which makes me sick.

I heard her one night talking
to Dad and saying that she wished
José would have told the head priest
instead of going to the police,
which is high-key fucked up
if you ask me.

But of course, no one asks me
because no one looks at me/talks to me.

I can't tell if it's the trans thing
or something else?

There are more people coming
forward all the time about
the abuse at Holy Guardian Angels.

José talked to me for
the first time in a while.

We were on opposite ends
of the sofa while Mom and Dad
were on their anniversary dinner
(they just went to an Olive Garden,
which is kind of sad but
at least they left the house).

He started, "Did anything ever happen
to you there?"

He didn't have to set up
context or anything.

I knew he was talking about church.

I had been an altar server
for two years.

"No, but one time
Noah told me that he wouldn't
go in the sacristy alone."

José started crying.

I moved closer to him.

I don't think I'd ever seen
him cry before.

I cried, too.

I said, "I'm sorry, I wish
it had been me."

He shook his head.
He asked, "Why would you say that?"

I didn't know.
It's just how
I feel when bad things
happen to other people. I just
always wish it was me.

Maybe that's bad
I don't know.

I just said, "Because I wish
it didn't happen to anyone."

We didn't say anything else
for a while and then he told
me what the priests did to him.

*His face was red, hot
to the touch, like a stove top.*

He was angry and heartbroken.

*He said, "I don't know
if I still believe in God."*

That made me sadder than anything

*because the only reason I ever
believed in God*

was him.

*Without our parents
it was like we could finally say
everything we'd been thinking.*

*I told José I've been jealous
that my parents believe him
but not me.*

José asked, "Believe what?"

*And I told him I'm his brother—
that I'm really his little brother.*

*José hugged me
and told me he's lucky
to have a brother like me.
He asked me what he could do
to help me
and the worst part*

*was I have no idea
what I need yet.*

*I don't know how
to end this letter.*

I care about you so much, Oliver

*I'll send you more pictures
of some illustrations
I'm working on*

—Aaron

OLIVER'S WINDOW I

From you:

[Image of a boy and another boy
on opposite sides of a canvas.
Between them is an ocean
with spirals of color,
rainbows and deep pinks and blues—
they swirl to reveal all types of purple:
lavenders and indigos and eggplant purples.
The sky is full of great dark birds,
their feathers dropping like leaves from trees.
The one boy tries to catch them.
The other boy holds a paintbrush
and he paints the ocean between them.]

OLIVER'S WINDOW II

You (Aaron): i want to call this painting "Oliver's Window."
I decided that years after the war is over
and the United States begins,
Aaron searches till he finds
Oliver's old window from their hometown
and he paints it.

He paints it over and over again as long as they
are apart.

Every week. I'm going to paint your window.

You (Aaron): im sorry im not always around to talk/text.

You (Aaron): i do want to be your partner or boyfriend
or whatever we call it.
im just worried we're going
to end up so far away from
each other that we'll end up
too different to know each other
anymore.

DIFFERENT

Me (Oliver): we're always different though.

Me (Oliver): we'd be changing even
if we just lived up the street
from each other.

WHAT TO SAY

Me (Oliver): im writing your letter for this week
which means it's kind of stupid
to text you but i wanted to

Me (Oliver): i guess what i should say is
i'm trying to write your letter
and failing at it

Me (Oliver): ive been thinking about
the soldiers

i wonder what they could
talk about in letters

maybe they ran out
        of new ideas to say

did they feel lost?

out of love?

i don't feel out of love but
i do feel

like im floating

i think about them so much
        it's ridiculous

maybe it's because you're
the only person i talk to about them

i could tell mom but she wouldn't
really get it

do you think
sometimes they lied to each other?

not real lies . . . just, like, made up stories

to entertain each other

i want to do that for you but
all i can think about

is how much i want to see you

and how i wouldn't have come
out without you . . .

i worry sometimes that
you think i copied you or something

i know that's dumb

but i worry

i haven't done enough

did they talk about running away together?

im sorry for all the texts

you can just respond in your letter

i appreciate you

we can do it

you can do it

i love you

WORLD WAR II

Dear Aaron, I write,

*I was happy to
finish the World War II unit.*

*Dad wouldn't stop asking
to help me study.*

*Before the test he called it
"father-son" time*

*which felt strange but
somewhat satisfying.*

*I don't know if
I'm ready for that(?)*

I don't know how to explain that
I want him to see me as a son
but that it feels like
it happened too fast.

He wanted to help me study
details that aren't important
like the names of firearms
and planes.

Mr. Claus believes it's more
important to study "culture and politics"

which Dad says are "implied."

I wasn't sure what he meant.

He said, "To people hurt by history,
the 'culture' or whatever
is easy to understand.
Of course, we know what
happened in World War II,
that's why I look at the planes
and the guns and tanks. Those
are things I don't know."

I didn't know what to say.

I wanted to call you
and ask you what you thought about that.

On the last day of studying
he was reading over a study guide
and he paused on a question.

He held the paper closer
and straightened it out.

"I didn't know that," he said.

"What?" I asked.

He said, "That they killed
gay people in the Holocaust too. I guess
I always thought it was only Jewish people and Romani."

"I think they don't usually
teach about it because there were
probably less gay
and trans people than
the other groups."

He looked at me.
"That's still important.
There were probably many gay and trans Jewish people
back then too.
I don't think I've ever
thought about that."

Realizing there was
something he didn't know
about World War II made him
act different the whole time
we studied.

I felt like he was listening to me!

It reminded me
that we have a lot
we can teach our parents
if they make time to listen.

—Oliver

WORLD HISTORY

Dear Oliver,

you write,

*In my new school we're
studying world history and
no one plays* Call of Duty *in class.*

*But that doesn't mean people pay attention.
Class is SO BORING.
The teacher puts on a slideshow every day
and turns off the lights.*

*Like literally how is one expected
not to conk the fuck out?*

*Sometimes when I'm sitting in class
I wonder if even YOU would be bored.
Haha but you might still like it
after all, you read
those dry freaking history books.*

*Ryan is still like my only friend
and we only share art class.*

*I know I could try to make more friends
but I can never tell
if people are going to accept that I'm a dude.
Not everyone has
a queer pride pin.*

It stresses me out like all the time.

*I'll be sitting in class and hear people laughing
and my brain is like
"They could be laughing at you."*

So, in classes like world history
I just kind of zone out.
Try not to sleep. Try not to get in trouble.
Try to focus and take some notes.

I know it's important
and I know I should care but
I'm not even staying here a full year
and it's our LAST YEAR.

I considered starting the video game up myself
but I didn't want to be the new kid getting
everyone in trouble.

We're learning about the Napoleonic Wars
BORING.

I'm literally dying. Dead even.

If you were here maybe you'd
find some lesbian queens or something.

Sometimes, I wonder
what other countries learn about us.

Probably more than we learn! Ha!

I was just thinking about how in elementary school
our fifth-grade teacher
was like,
"Some slave owners were nice to their slaves."

Like what the fuck is that???

You can't "be nice" to someone you're enslaving!

I wonder if one day they'll learn
about child abuses at churches like mine too

and think that all the people at the churches
were terrible.

The worst part about everything
is that some people, mainly my mom,
say it's because

the priests were gay,

the ones who molested all those kids
and José.

I get so furious
that I want to tear myself apart.

I think of me and you and
all the queer people out there.

There's so much love.

I'm sorry this got dark,
I just haven't gotten
to talk to anyone about this.

Ryan is really nice to talk to
but sometimes I'm scared
if I vent to them they'll be like
"Damn, Aaron is a lot to deal with."

I don't tell people at my new school
why we moved.

Who wants to be known
for his brother being
a victim of sexual assault?

I tell Ryan that we moved
because my dad got a promotion,

which is totally a lie because
Mom and Dad miss their jobs
they had in Kutztown.

Ryan is great but they don't
always understand.

Their parents
are just so supportive.

Their parents literally started a group
for people with nonbinary kids!

It's not that I want someone else
having a hard time with their parents

but it sucks when you're surrounded
by people with families like that.

I guess at least José is there for me.

I'm sorry this was just
a sad rambling.

You're great.

I'll send you more pictures
When I work on them.

Tell me something nice
about history

when you get the chance.

Also also

What are you doing for Christmas break?

Maybe you could visit here.

I told Ryan about you
and they were like "You have to bring him here
so we can go on a queer tour of the city all together!"

Ryan said, "Maybe seeing Oliver happy
and out as a trans person
could help show your parents
what being trans really is."

I'm a little skeptical about it being that easy
but hey who knows—
anything's possible I guess.

I've had a hard time making this place
feel like a home

but with you it could
be like at least an adventure

I don't think my parents would care.

I'm not sure if they would
call you "Oliver" though because
they still think you're [****].

I didn't tell them you're a boy
and I'm sorry I didn't.

Would you want me to?

I should have but I'm worried they'll
think I want to be a boy
because you want to be a boy

when really we just
both happen to be boys.

Anyway,

Aaron

THE 1960S

Dear Aaron, I write,

The topic for my paper
is the gay rights movement
in the late 1960s.

It's perfect that you just
asked about some moment

in history because
that's what I'm writing about
right now.

I feel bad because Dad just
started reading Revolutionary War
books to "bond" and I'm not really

as into that right now. Of course
I care about the soldiers,
            our soldiers,

but I never even knew
anything about people just like us
in the 1960s, so it feels
new and exciting!

Actually there were gay societies
even earlier than the 1960s!
But I'm doing
research on that time for my paper.

Basically,
they got sick of being treated

terribly and they rose up
and fought back.

We have all the rights we do
probably because of them—transgender people
like us! Well, actually more specifically
trans women of color—
but trans people! Rising up!!!
Fighting police!

It makes me feel like
revolutions are still possible.

I'm sorry, I'm getting
ahead of myself.

I barely even described
who "they" are . . .
were, I guess.

Well . . . actually
some are probably still alive.

Have you ever thought about that?

There are people alive now
who were alive when
just being gay was illegal.

First thing was the Stonewall Riots.
They were like a huge tipping point
for gay rights.

These cops tried to raid a gay bar.
They attacked and hurt the queer people inside
but the queer people didn't give up.
They rioted. They fought back!

This sparked years of queer organizing.
Of course, queer people were organizing

before Stonewall but now
we were finally visible!

Sometimes I feel weird saying "we."
I never read about trans men specifically
but I believe we were there. I have to.

Black trans women were the first
to spark the riots. Some historians
attribute the first brick thrown
to Marsha P. Johnson.

Imagine being a trans woman
in the 1960s! We should learn more
about people like her in school.
Marginalized even in queer communities
but still fighting for equality.

She and her friend Sylvia Rivera
started an organization called STAR
to support young homeless
drag queens, gay youth, and trans women in the city.

This reminds me that even in the hardest times
we can find ways to uplift each other.

Know I'm always here for you
and I wish I could hold you right now.

I love you,

Oliver

THE LETTER MAILED BUT I DIDN'T WANT TO WAIT TO TELL YOU

Me (Oliver): so i tried to fit everything in my letter but
i forgot to say that i do want to come over during

winter break. i think about you so much, i'm
scared that when i see you all i'll want to do
is kiss you and i don't want you to get
in trouble with your parents, you know? i wish
we were older

Me (Oliver): i know this is crazy but i imagine our whole
lives together. i imagine an apartment in the city
and the morning sun in the window, you rolling
over and me getting up early to make you pancakes
only it wouldn't be all messed up like it was that
last sleepover. i still feel bad about that.

Me (Oliver): i have been wanting to tell you other things too.
i think about you in other ways too. i don't want
to be weird, i just think about touching you, i think
about how my heart quickens when i think
of you and i wish we had had more sleepovers here,
i want to learn about your body, all of it.

Me (Oliver): do you remember that one time this summer?
you were on top of me and we were kissing
on the hill at the edge of town, the smell of freshly
cut grass on the breeze. you got on top of me
and each kiss took me deeper and deeper into myself.
i felt like i could love the parts of my body
that i usually can't stand
when they were touching you because you
always see me for who i am,
like somehow your lips sucking my neck could
make my gender real

COMIC PANELS II

You, Aaron, send:

> [Image of a wall where
> each stone is a different color,
> not just a rainbow
> but a kaleidoscope, whirling,
> almost like flecks of confetti on stone.]

> [Image of a grassy hill in summer.
> The green is the shade of lime rinds
> and spearmint gum.]

> [Image of an eye: close up.
> The eye is brown but up close
> you can see all the little strands
> of color meandering through it.]

You (Aaron): when i think of that afternoon all i think
of is your eyes, i looked at them and forgot we had bodies.

You (Aaron): if you come over during break i'll find a place
for us to go like the hill.

TEXTING

> *Dear Oliver,*

you write,

> *I tried to write
> this letter a few times.*

> *Each time I didn't think
> about the soldiers.*

I was just focused on explaining

then I tried to think about
what they would say to each other and
it made more sense.

I guess what I want to
say is that I'm sorry
I haven't talked to you.

I keep pushing everyone away,
that's why I didn't want to
text you or you to text me.

I wanted to seal myself up.

I wanted to live in an envelope,
dissolve into a pile of unsaid words.

I thought that if we wrote
letters we could drift slowly away
from each other.

It would hurt less like that
I thought.

I don't want to move apart
from you.

Do you still think about me?

I know you'll say yes
but I have to ask.

I don't know what we
are without all our old places.

I can't imagine you
in this new world:

the gray of the streets, the wind
between the skyscrapers.

You belong in grassy fields,
bunk beds,
and elm trees.

I want to show you this place,
I really do. I talk to Ryan all the time about you.
Sometimes José even asks how you are
and I always kind of
make something up.

How could I tell them
how much being away from you hurts?

I think if the soldiers
had cell phones
(how funny does that sound?)

they would call each other
every night,

maybe they would walk

away from their homes, from

the cabins,

the glowing screen pressed
to the side of their face,

speaking in a whisper.

Maybe they would say

"I miss you."

I miss you, Oliver,
I fucking miss you.

I bet the soldiers would have had to hide
missing each other
because no one would understand
that they weren't just friends—
that they were in love.

I bet they felt
as lonely as I do.

Look, you have me
writing like you.

You have me on
about dead
colonial soldiers.

What could they know about us?
Really?
Do you really think
there were trans soldiers?

I don't know if I do.

Text me
Text me
Text me

—Aaron

SILENCES

[UNSENT LETTER]

Dear Oliver,

Today Mom and Dad and José and I
were watching a football game (yuck)

during a commercial
I thought I'd ask
if maybe you could visit.

I said, "I miss my friend from Kutztown . . .
Maybe they could like come and check out the city
sometime."

I don't know why
I didn't just say Oliver.

Mom and Dad shared a look
that I knew meant
they were judging something
about what I said.

Mom asked, "What friend?"
even though, like me, she had to know
I was talking about you.

"****," I said, using your other name
because she might not
have remembered "Oliver."

Dad got up to go to the kitchen,
which is always a sign
he wants Mom to handle something.

Mom pretended to be watching the TV extra intently,
acting almost distracted.
She said, "Well, you know
you can't have sleepovers
here in this house."

That wasn't something she'd said before—
but still she was talking around what she meant,
which was

"You're not allowed
to have your partner stay over" or maybe
"We don't like Oliver."

I don't know what they think
we would even do?

It's not like you not being here
makes me any less trans
or any less gay.

I feel defeated
but at the same time

I'm scared if I challenge her
I'll ruin any chance
of Mom and Dad understanding.

I wish José
would have said something
but he seemed
at a loss for words too.

Please know,
I care about you so much
and I wanted to stand up to my family for you—
for us.

I just don't know
if I know how to yet.

—Aaron

PLANS I

Me (Oliver): hi, what are you up to?

Me (Oliver): My mom is being weird
about letting me take the bus up
to see you.

Me (Oliver): i just think we need like
a plan or something, some way
that she'll let me go?

Me (Oliver): i just really want to see you.

PLANS II

You (Aaron): so what if José
comes to pick you up in our family's car?
He's like
an adult, right?
Maybe I could talk him into it.

Me (Oliver): i don't know if my parents would trust him
and that's super far?? I would feel bad.

You (Aaron): José is like the most
trustworthy person ever

Me (Oliver): i know but like i don't
know if my parents would think that

Me (Oliver): it has nothing to do with José
i just want to make sure my parents
let me go

You (Aaron): okay

PLANS III

Me (Oliver): what if your parents got me from
the station when i get off?

You (Aaron): i don't know.
im sorry im just freaking out a little . . .
i don't know if i can like talk to them right now
i feel really nervous

Me (Oliver): oh! im sorry i didn't
mean to be pushy

You (Aaron): i know! you weren't
i just get so worried about adding something
else to everything, like adding you
into the mix

Me (Oliver): they don't know we're dating
though right?

You (Aaron): im scared if i ask about
you coming over
they'll know like for sure and they'll like
never let anyone come over . . .
we could just wait a little longer

Me (Oliver): you could have told
me that sooner!

Me (Oliver): I'm sorry for like bothering

Me (Oliver): were you just planning
to like hide me when i come?

                              You (Aaron): i haven't figured
                                        out the details yet.

Me (Oliver): you could come here!
Well, i mean my parents wouldn't
let us share a room but we could hang out.

                              You (Aaron): i don't know if my parents
                                        would let me, they're acting all
                                        excited about the holidays
                                        and they haven't been excited
                                        about anything for so long
                                        and with the moving and
                                        the church and everything
                                        i'm sorry. it's like my mom got
                                        out the decorations and our
                                        house has poinsettias all over
                              you know all the colors mom gets

Me (Oliver): that's great!

                              You (Aaron): i'm sorry Oliver

Me (Oliver): about what?

                              You (Aaron): that its not going
                                        to work out

Me (Oliver): wait, when did we say that?

You (Aaron): i thought i said, you know

Me (Oliver): i didn't get that from what you said.

You (Aaron): from what?

Me (Oliver): what you said?
You mean your parents wouldn't
want me around even if it's
not like Christmas? i can
make sure it's a different day

You (Aaron): your parents won't
even let you come though

You (Aaron): it's easy for you to ask these
things, your parents actually try to
understand you and you forget that mine
aren't even close to doing that

You (Aaron): they aren't like yours

SELF

Dear Oliver (writing to myself),

I think I don't like myself,
at least not right now.

On the first day I went to the therapist
she told me I should write

to myself.

I thought that sounded dumb
so I just wrote to Aaron
over and over and over.

I'm writing to you, self,
because I should have written sooner.

Sometimes I wonder if I'm real.

I guess not sometimes,
all the time.

Not my gender anymore,
but my whole self,

and I think that's because you
can love someone else so much

that you start to erase yourself

and you start to try to
erase them.

I feel so sorry.

I'm not going to tell the therapist
any of this because that would
be melodramatic and

I don't want to talk about
it any more than this.

This is just for us.
This year Chanukkah felt routine:

Mom taking out the blue menorah and
setting it on the windowsill.

Dad making sufganiyot on
the first night.

I pulled apart
the golden brown dough and
chewed slowly.

Each night, a light.

It felt like any other week
this year
because I'm not enjoying
the holiday, I'm just
missing Aaron.
I remembered being little
and looking so forward
to it, as if it might never happen again.
Now everything feels routine
without Aaron.

I didn't text Aaron back.

I didn't.

I don't know why.

I just felt like
he doesn't see me as real either.

Not my gender, I mean
everything.

I know I'll feel differently
after a while, but right now

I'm a soldier writing to
Aaron from the past

a grassy hill

a mouth.

Trying to love you,

Oliver

CANCELED PLANS

Mom: you haven't come downstairs
The aunts are here.
We're going to have dinner soon.

Oliver: i don't feel like it right now, is that okay?

Mom: They only have enough time off to come
once or twice a year . . . I'm sure they're excited to see you . . .

Oliver: I really don't feel like it.

Mom: well i made dinner and
your aunts are waiting.

Mom: Come on we can even play a board game after dinner!

Mom: i talked to them, remember i told you?
we talked on thanksgiving.
i explained the whole thing, they're going
to call you your name and everything
or at least they'll try. they support you.

Oliver: Thank you

Mom: Well if you can't come down that's okay
but i did make butternut squash . . .

Oliver: hmmm tempting.

Mom: can i ask you something?

Oliver: ???

Mom: Does this have to do with
Aaron? i know you were trying
to figure out something for break

Oliver: it didn't work out

Mom: well that's a shame.
Maybe he could visit here sometime.

Oliver: if his parents let him

Mom: i see

Oliver: i'll come down eventually

Oliver: what do you do when
you should have listened
to someone better?

Mom: you tell them that.

Mom: Like remember when I asked
you too many questions that
one night after your therapist's appointment?

Oliver: Yeah and i freaked out

Mom: and i texted you
to tell you i was sorry i was so focused
on my own understanding that
i stopped listening to
what you needed

Oliver: ah its so weird that
my mom is cool

Mom: ☺

Oliver: yep, the emoji ruined it

NO PHONES AT THE TABLE

Aaron: ugh i miss holidays in town.

José: and we thought they were big there!

Aaron: i don't know like half the table,
is that kid wearing the silver bow tie
from mom's side or dad's side?

José: i don't know

Aaron: is this a kids table?

José: i'm goin to call it the "halfway" table
because Tío is here so it's like almost adults

Aaron: ew im an almost adult?

José: i wouldn't go that far ☺

Aaron: i want it to be over

José: you look, like, dead, it's Christmas?
What's wrong?

Aaron: i feel stupid. It's complicated.

José: girl problems?

Aaron: haha . . . no
boy problems.
Everything problems.

José: it was a joke i know you told me
about Oliver ☺

Aaron: oh yeah . . . haha duh.
im just like always on the defensive im sorry

José: don't be sorry i get it!

Aaron: i just wish i was
out of here and i know i messed up.

José: how so?

Aaron: i invited Oliver
to Christmas here even though
i knew i wouldn't get the courage
to really push mom / dad to let him stay here
i got all worried about how
mom and dad would react
if i brought it up again
and everyone's still dealing
with the move and
all the other stuff

José: you mean my stuff?

Aaron: it's not just your stuff though
Everyone's clearly treating me different
since I started dressing more masculine.

Aaron: did you see yesterday
mom set out those two pictures of me
in the fluffy pink dress from easter a few years ago?
they're high key silently fighting my transness
every free moment they have

José: hey, im sorry

Aaron: for what?
You're like the only person
not being weird about it.

José: yeah but i haven't tried
to help either. i don't know how to yet
but i will.

José: also . . . you should have invited him,
no one would notice him in
all this chaos

Aaron: haha of course they
would he's the palest person
i think i've ever known

José: ohhhh true true

José: Can I ask you something?

Aaron: sure??

José: What would you want me to say
like if I talk to mom and dad
about you?

Aaron: wow that's hard.
i mean really i just want them
to fucking understand
this is just who i am
it's not something other people made me.
sometimes i think they think being trans is like
not something people like us do . . .
but it is! im real and i just want to feel
like part of this family again.

Aaron: why did they believe you
and not me?

José: i get that . . . i'll try
to think of a way to slip that into conversation
haha with different wording obviously!!

José: thanks for trusting me

Aaron: thanks for being
a great brother . . .

ugh now i feel all weepy
going to the bathroom BRB!

WINTER BREAK POEM I

[UNSENT LETTER]

Dear Oliver,

*If I die in this cold winter
valley*

*will you remember me
as we were this last summer
in town*

*with the flowers blooming
on the crests of the green hills*

*and the light scent
of sun in our hair?*

I love you,

*Aaron
1778*

WINTER BREAK POEM II

[UNSENT LETTER]

Dear Oliver,

*If I die in the cold winter
valley*

will you remember me?

*Will you remember me as who I was
and not as the person
who didn't come back*

*and left you for a war
none of us understand?*

I love you,

*Aaron
1778*

WINTER BREAK POEM III

[UNSENT LETTER]

Dear Oliver,

The truth is,

*I don't know if I'll love
you*

when I see you.

I'm scared of hurting you.

I'm scared of the terrible
things that happen to people
like us.

I'm scared of not
being real enough for you.

I'm scared of God.

I'm scared of my mom.

I'm scared of how quiet my dad is now.

I'm scared of knowing you
in a new place.

I'm scared I won't
want to spend

my life with you.

I'm scared I'm changing.

I'm scared I'm not in control of how I'm changing.

Do you understand?

I don't want
to hurt you.

I love you,
I really do love you,

Aaron

WINTER BREAK LETTER

Dear Oliver,

Do you remember how
last year on the very last day

of winter break we started the day
by going to the dollar store
and buying super cheap Christmas candy?

I loved that. We ate so much of it
and you laughed and said you'd
never be able to be vegan because
you like milk chocolate too much
and I said I'd never think about going vegan
because I like food too much.

After that you came over and sat
on the couch and watched me play Kingdom Hearts,
which I don't even really like that much
but you liked watching me play.
I had to get out my old PlayStation 2 to show you.

What I don't think I've ever told
you is I don't play video games alone,
like ever. It's fucking lonely, really lonely.

I hate it.

I tried to play Kingdom Hearts today
because I wanted to remember last year
but I couldn't because I felt like
an asshole for talking about
seeing you and then just trailing off.

It's scary, Oliver, it's scary.
It's not that I feel stuck with you,
but more like I feel so entwined
with you that I'm scared to let myself
be that close again.

We practically
named each other.

I don't really know who I am
or if this new place is making me different.

Do you ever regret your name?

I love my name but I wish
I would have waited longer,
then again I could spend
forever changing my mind.
I hope this doesn't come
off wrong, Oliver, I just
wanted to let you know
what I've really been thinking.

I care about you so much.

If I were to talk to you
I'd have so many stories
about school.

I'm quieter
in my new school. You'd be surprised.

Would you recognize me now?

I don't know.

I got a rejection letter
from an art school I applied to.

There's still a bunch more
but I wonder what I'll do
if I don't get in anywhere.

I'm scared of being stuck here.

I'm scared I'm becoming
less and less myself
each day I'm away from you

and the creek and my family's real
house that's not even ours anymore.

Have you thought about
where you'll go next year?

Have you heard
from anywhere?

You can be anything but

you should also be a history teacher

but like specializing
in queer history.

You just are really good at it,

you make me feel like
I have existed before

and I can get through this.

You can text me,

—Aaron

COMIC PANELS III

You (Aaron):

[Image of a heart, purple like a bruise.
The heart is coming out of an envelope.]

[Image of a boy holding
the heart and letting it out.
The boy is standing alone
on a rock by a creek.]

[Image of the heart sprouting
moth wings and fluttering just above the water.]

NEW YEAR'S

I write,

Dear Aaron,

I went to the dollar store alone
and I got the same gross milk chocolates
with the crunchy middles
and I couldn't really finish them
on my own.

I was thinking about last year, too.

I've said this before
but I really think it's okay

that we keep changing.

We will be different,

it's kind of inevitable.

I just realized today that we're
in a New Year and
it's always been weird
to me that the New Year

is halfway through
the school year.

We're halfway through
our senior year and

we've already changed so much.

I haven't even seen you this year.

Do you have the same haircut?

You never update your
Instagram

I want to see you

I just don't know
when it would be right

for you
and for me
to see each other.

Do you want to see me?

I get worried that we'll

never

talk

again.

After graduation, though,
we'll both be eighteen
and it won't matter,

right?

We could do whatever we want.

We could even go and do
a real reenactment together
and be like our soldiers!

I've actually really been
enjoying working
on my reenacting stuff.

I made you a costume
You don't ever have to wear it.

I made it a while ago
and then I felt bad about
it so I just stuck the thing
in the back of my closet.

I told my dad that it was a spare
one for me.

I don't know why
I wanted to tell
you that, I just felt
like I needed to.

Happy New Year!
Love you!

—Oliver

A POEM WITHOUT YOU

One morning before school,
imagining our soldiers,
      I write, *Dear Aaron,*

Even if we both survive the war
I know there is a chance
we won't see each other again.

I want you to know
I will carry your name inside me—
a continuous echo, and in each repetition
will flicker a different moment
I am missing you.

Dear Aaron, I hope there are enough supplies
for your regiment. I hope

you have found new friends
among the men there.

Love,

Oliver
1778

CASIMIR PULASKI

Dear Aaron, I write

Today I'm thinking about uncertainty
as I finish reading a story today online
about a general from the American Revolution
named Casimir Pulaski.

Recently historians dug up his skeleton
to do research and found his bones
were more like typical "female" bones.
Some people argued we should just assume
this was someone else's body.

Other people said it's possible
he was female. How amazing is that?
He might have even been intersex,
which is a term for people whose biological sex characteristics
fall somewhere between male and female.
I know there's still that chance the body isn't his
but I'm not going to read any more.
I know he's an intersex trans man
and he existed all those years ago.
He even has a holiday named after him!

I think uncertainty is a part of history
and maybe we need uncertainty also to understand

the future. Ugh, my brain is just
in knots. Is it wrong to decide
a historical figure is queer?

I think we need to—we decide
so many are cis and straight without question.

Love,

Oliver

AFTER GRADUATION

Me (Oliver): can i tell you a crazy idea i had?

You (Aaron): what?

Me (Oliver): its stupid

You (Aaron): you can't bring something up and just
like not tell me???

Me (Oliver): i think after graduation
we should meet up but not before then

Me (Oliver): we should meet up
after graduation and we should
like actually go and reenact together

You (Aaron): what? How would that
even work you think my mom would let
me around people firing guns?
Even if they're fake she'd FLIP.

Me (Oliver): you like turned 18,
and my birthday is next month in March.

Me (Oliver): You're an adult
you can do whatever you want.

                    You (Aaron): i have no clue how i'd keep
                    an overnight trip from my parents
                    they're not just going to be like
                    okay see ya later!

Me (Oliver): okay so we tell them we're going
with friends from Kutztown on senior week
to the beach

Me (Oliver): that's reasonable

                    You (Aaron): that could
                    maybe work

Me (Oliver): in the meantime
we save our money
for an Uber there or a bus maybe . . .
Do you think they have buses to
reenactment places?

                    You (Aaron): hotels?

Me (Oliver): Oh we'd just sleep in a tent

                    You (Aaron): . . .

Me (Oliver): its romantic.

                    You (Aaron): you want us to celebrate
                    graduating by sleeping in a muddy field
                    and running around pretending
                    like we're Revolutionary War soldiers?

Me (Oliver): i know but i feel like
we have to

Me (Oliver): like it will help

You (Aaron): ugh

You (Aaron): i do too

Me (Oliver): you can change your mind too

You (Aaron): no i want to
im just scared

Me (Oliver): i am too

You (Aaron): and we can figure
out there if we like . . .

You (Aaron): you know?

Me (Oliver): still love each other?

You (Aaron): yeah

You (Aaron): im sorry

Me (Oliver): its okay
we should

TESTOSTERONE NIGHTMARES

Me (Oliver):

I had this dream last night that you had found testosterone, like
    ordered it illegally online
which is funny because that's totally not something you would
    do. You kept telling me
that we needed to try it, that we should take it together. I kept
    telling you that I was scared
and that I wasn't sure if it would change me and if I wanted to
    be changed yet. You held

my arm tight and told me I needed to, that we needed to do this
together.

Me (Oliver): I don't usually draw but I thought I would try to
send you a drawing for once.

Me (Oliver): I'm sorry if it's weird.

Me (Oliver): The dream isn't your fault, it's just my own stuff.
Sometimes
I just feel like I'm not a boy enough
because you're so much more masculine than me.
Like, even in how you dress. I never dressed like you.
No one would have called me a tomboy.

Me (Oliver): Look at me spilling all my baggage
I just meant to show you my drawings . . .

[Image of a boy holding a needle:
The needle is huge, like a giant glinting saber.]

[Image of a boy plunging the needle
into another boy, into his chest.
Blood trickles from the wound:
a crimson ribbon.]

TESTOSTERONE DREAMS I

You (Aaron): Nothing could make either
of us more a man than the other

You (Aaron): if testosterone is all
that makes someone a man,
then what would be the point?

TESTOSTERONE DREAMS II

Me (Oliver): Maybe I'll be able to decide after we go

You (Aaron): if you want to try taking
testosterone or not?

Me (Oliver): yeah

You (Aaron): Maybe you can ask
the other soldiers' opinions ☺

Me (Oliver): I just might!

BATTLE OF MONMOUTH

Me (Oliver): so i've been researching reenactments and
one battle right after the troops stayed at Valley Forge
was the Battle of Monmouth

Me (Oliver): I was thinking maybe our soldiers
might have fought in that
maybe they marched there together

You (Aaron): Where's that?
Me (Oliver): It's like a whole festival!

You (Aaron): WHERE?

Me (Oliver): Oh, sorry didn't see that
It's in New Jersey!
it's like the perfect time right in June!

You (Aaron): And people camp out?
I'm sorry I know it's dumb I'm just
all worried we're actually doing this.

Me (Oliver): Yeah and it's not too expensive
to sign up to reenact.

Me (Oliver): We don't have to
I know it would be hard to figure out.

You (Aaron): I don't know if I know enough
to be our soldiers.

You (Aaron): I don't know if I know them
as much as you do.

Me (Oliver): Enough?

You (Aaron): You know like
I just want to do them justice.
I don't know if I'm even like the people who fought.

You (Aaron): Were there even
Puerto Rican people
at this battle?

Me (Oliver): I'm sure there could have been!
Also . . . just because historians didn't write about it
doesn't mean there weren't.
We get missed by history.
I have to believe going to the reenactment
is like honoring people like us
who aren't in paintings and history books.

You (Aaron): Hmm I actually kind of like that
I'm gonna do some more research tonight also.

Me (Oliver): Me too!! You're excited, aren't you?

You (Aaron): Ugh, yeah I am.

MAYBE

Me (Oliver):
I know this might not all work out
Maybe, even after the trip, we'll grow apart
Maybe we won't tell our new friends in college the story of how
    we got our names
Maybe we'll forget each other, slowly, not all at once
Maybe we won't hold hands again or share cheap chocolates
Maybe we'll get lost on the trip to the battlefield in the rolling
    fields of corn and soybeans
Maybe our words too will get lost there, becoming paint in our
    mouths
Maybe we will have to communicate by making pictures, our
    faded love stamped into canvas
Maybe we'll never know if trans people existed in the Revolution
    like how I imagine our soldiers
Maybe we'll see them reflected in more stories but never how we
    understand them
Maybe they're make-believe
Maybe the idea is just meant to comfort us, to comfort me
Maybe I love history and I want it to help me understand myself
But despite it all I want you to remember
that we existed and we loved each other so much
that we existed and maybe someday us existing
will give someone else hope

WE'RE HISTORY

You (Aaron): I've been thinking about the soldiers.
    Ha! It feels like I always am. Sometimes
    they just arise in my brain
    when I don't feel like any of this is worth it.

It feels like if someone back then
could survive as queer
and we an imagine their queerness
all these years later then maybe
they'll understand ours.

You (Aaron): I know this is dumb but
thanks for telling me about the soldiers,
I don't know what I would
do without them sometimes.
I think we don't thank people enough
for trusting us with their imaginations.

You (Aaron): How weird is that?
I miss people I never knew.

You (Aaron): I miss people
who we invented.

You (Aaron): Not invented—
discovered!

Me (Oliver): It pays to have a history-buff boyfriend ☺

1.4 MILLION QUIET REVOLUTIONS

I write, *Dear Aaron,*

A few nights ago
you said "I don't know what I would
do without them."

I wanted to tell you that a few days ago
I decided to figure out how many people

in the United States are trans
and most estimates say
about 1.4 million people.

Do you know how many people
fought in the Revolutionary War?

Not even a million!

I've been thinking that I don't
really know what the word revolution
is supposed to mean.

What revolution did that war actually bring?

Revolution is supposed to mean
rebellion, revolt, change, mutiny,
and transformation.

What is more revolutionary
than all those trans people's
wonderful
brilliant
vibrant
unique

lives?

We're linked to them

even if we only know
a few trans people

in real life.

Even if we have to carve out
our history.

Even if people say we're silly years later
for running away
together for a weekend to

make real these soldiers
we dreamed of.

—Oliver

III

BATTLEFIELD

OTHER GIRLS

The older I get the more
I admit to myself that I'm not
as much of a badass as I'd like to think.

That's how I see myself or at least
that's how I saw myself:
like this hard-core dyke.

Since I figured out I'm a man
it's all been mixed up.

Suddenly, I don't feel so much
like a fist.
I don't loathe the color pink.

I used to always say to people
in middle school,
"I'm not like other girls—
other girls are annoying and
always have so much drama."

What an asshole.

I wasn't a girl at all
and my defense
was putting down girls altogether.

I was resisting
being the kind of girl
Mom and Dad wanted me to be.

The kind of girl
with hands folded in her lap

and ribbons in her hair
and white Sunday-school shoes
and legs crossed
wearing a knee-length dress.

There is still a picture at the end of the hallway
in our apartment
taken when I was in fifth grade
and José was in middle school.

My hair is long and wavy and brown,
falling around my face.
I have my hands clasped
one in the other.

Each day when I pass the picture
I don't see myself—
I see a different person entirely.

In the picture, José's arm is around me—
touching my shoulder.
Behind us stand Mom and Dad.
All of us smiling.

Was this ever really
a picture of us?
Was I ever happy
as a girl?
Now I really feel like
there isn't anything wrong
with being feminine or girly—
it's just not for me.

I still wonder sometimes
what made me different.

When I tell José
that sometimes I wish I knew why I'm trans
he tells me
the reason won't ever matter to him
because he loves me
for who I am.

How is it that José
is the same as he was in the picture
and I am so different?

THE END OF THE YEAR

I can't believe there's a part of me
who still misses Kutztown.
My new school is like an amazing 180.

I like actually have friends who are girls
and nonbinary people.
At Kutztown, I wanted to prove I was a guy
by only having friends who were guys
which was kinda gender affirming at the time,
but it's even better to get to know other queer people.

It's also kind of ridiculous when you think about it—
like obviously you can have friends of all genders?

Honestly, I have Ryan to thank for that.
Every day they would be, like,
"Dude, you have to come to Spectrum."
(Spectrum is the LGBTQIA+ group at school.)
I kept being, like,
"No, you know I have to go do homework,"
or "My parents want me home."
Which, yeah, they did,

but I could easily have told them
I had a club after school.

I guess I was worried
the group would be
1) all white kids
2) all people who had been out for longer than me
3) people who knew much more about being queer

Really, I just thought the group
might make me feel even more weird and lonely
and like I didn't belong anywhere.

It was totally not any of those things
which was fucking refreshing. I didn't know
queer groups like Spectrum existed.
I've learned so freaking much from my friends,
and I'm not the only Latino for once!

In fact, my friend Luz's family is from Colombia.
Luz taught me about nonbinary pronouns
and words in Spanish,
which by the way is super interesting.

One example is using *e* instead
of *o* or *a*
as an ending for words describing people—
so instead of *ella* or *él*,
Luz says *elle*.

It's exciting to learn that language is flexible
and that there are queer people who understand what it's like
to feel divided between your culture and your family
and your history
and your queerness.

At Kutztown I just
hung out with the guys
and really you and I only had each other.

You would love it here, Oliver.
I wish I could have stolen you
for this last semester.

Everyone from Spectrum
stands together to get pictures
in our caps and gowns.

The ceremony is going to start
in only an hour or so.

The school colors here are yellow
and green, which I think is an ugly combo.

Gloria has been determined
to get a selfie with every single teacher
and she catches me off guard as she
snaps one with me.

I realize I haven't texted you any pictures
of me at graduation.

A wave of missing you smacks me
and it feels wrong doing this
without you.

I realize a part of me
has always been imagining you here—
in Spectrum meetings
and history classes
and sitting in the park after school.

It takes this moment to remind me
I have a new life
that you're not here for.

THE LAST SPECTRUM
MEETING OF THE YEAR

All of us in the art room
sitting in a circle like we always did,
me next to Luz and Ryan.

I felt kind of sad
because I think I would be
such a different person

if I'd gone to this school
for all four years.
Like yes, I'm happy to be who I am

but this kind of space
is magical.
We always open

with a funny ice-breaker question,
and the president of Spectrum, a trans woman
named Lily, asked,

"If you had to live in a time period
other than the present,
when would you live?"

Around the circle
everyone had different answers
and I imagined all these trans people

in "Rome" and "ancient Egypt"
and "the Renaissance" and "the Meiji Period"
and "the American 1920s."

When it came to me, I thought of you
and I wanted to say,
"The American Revolution,"
but instead I said, "The future,"
and everyone snapped
and knocked on nearby tables.

IS IT POSSIBLE TO HAVE
TWO LIVES AT ONCE?

I feel like I've had at least
a dozen lives at this point.

One life as a girl
one life as your girlfriend
one life as a maybe boy and then a boy
and then a boy who lives in a tiny town
and a boy who lives in a big city
and a brother
and a boy who helps plan
a pride party with Spectrum
and a boy who starts coming out to teachers
with the help of his friends
and then a boy who everyone knows
is both a boy and trans
and now a boy who doesn't want to hide
being trans anymore
and a boy who misses you
and a boy who worries
that who I am now
isn't who I was
when we were together.

COLLISION

I realize our plans
are all laid for next week.

We're going to be in the same world again . . .
We're going to collide.

You'll tell me everything
that wouldn't fit in letters.

What haven't I told you?

I've like barely even told you
about my friends.

At least
so far, everything is set.

I hope this all works out.

"Hello, Earth to Aaron?"

Ryan waves their hand in front of my face.

"Sorry," I say.

They wiggle their eyebrows.
"You thinking about your little trip?"

"Yeah." I put my phone
back in my pocket

and stick out my tongue,
leaning into one of Gloria's selfies.

OUR COVER

Since Ryan is going to
the beach anyway with most of my friends

they agreed to be our cover.

It will be pretty simple: Everyone
just has to keep the story straight that
I'm going to Wildwood

with the rest of the group.
Pretty simple? I'll get
a bus to Kutztown
and just tell my mom
I'm leaving with friends
to drive to the beach in Jersey.

The truth is
I'm not good at lying.

Like I said, I like to think I'm badass
and then it comes down to the moment
and I can't take it.

Every time my parents ask more
questions about the "senior week trip"
I feel the anxiety building in me
like a fucking volcano.

There's no way in hell my parents
would let me go to a war reenactment
on my own,
let alone with you.

After everything with José
Mom sees every place we go

as a catastrophe
waiting to happen

and it's EXHAUSTING.

I'm a grown man—

which is still hard for me
to even say
but I am.

I'm eighteen.
I can make this decision.

I'm an adult now
and I can
decide things

On. My. Own.

OVERTIME

What sucks is
I know Mom means well.
I know she loves me. I know she feels like
she's holding the family together.

Mom and Dad both got jobs
at the hospital and they work
super ridiculous hours.
While I go to school
and José stays home splitting his days between
reading and trying to find a job.

It's so expensive
to live in the city.

Dad is too tired
to do basically anything but
eat
sleep and
repeat.

He nods off
watching reruns of football games
in the afternoons.

Some of Mom's shifts
are half of a whole day.
Twelve hours.
But she was still
cooking and cleaning
and doing laundry

until José and I started splitting it.

It's ridiculous that chores
are "gendered" but
I still felt weird
folding clothes and stuff.

I hate gender roles.
Like . . . why is it manly
not to clean and be clean?

On top of everything
Dad has been getting
overtime. I hardly ever
see them together.

I actually miss our
family dinners

and even going
to mass together.

I didn't like church
but I did like
being all together
and getting breakfast
at the diner in Kutztown afterward.

I guess a part of me feels kind of
abandoned.

We moved here for José and my parents
have even less time
to pay attention to me.

It's like everything they do
is to avoid talking about me being trans.

And I'm so proud to be trans
but there's so much more I want to talk about.
About my art
and my friends and
what new project ideas I have.

I know it sounds selfish
but I don't think it really is selfish
to want to feel
like a family.

MOM AND DAD

They've gotten really strict, too,
now that José is getting asked to be
interviewed all the time.

The priest's abuse story has
gotten more national attention,

which is good and bad.

Good:
Something will change
at that church
and hopefully at others.

Bad:
We can't seem
to get away from it.

News stations even want to interview me
and I don't have anything smart to say.

At the gym on the weekends
I'll sometimes glance up at the TV to see
the headlines: "Possibly Over 1,000 Victims
in Entire Diocese."

I try to just look away,
focusing on the treadmill track
spinning below me.

José tells me, "I wish I would
have tried to remain anonymous,
but then maybe the story wouldn't
have ever broken the way it did."

I say, "I'm sorry," because
sometimes that's all you can say.

I wish I could
dump more of my feelings
on him, but it doesn't always feel right
with everything he has going on.

José is always saying,
"Aaron, please. Tell me anything.
I want to be here for you."

But a part of me still feels like
my problems aren't as important as his.

ONE SUNDAY MORNING

I guess there are good moments too.
Mom, José, and me
got fresh bagels
at a bakery up the street.

We sat outside the shop
on wobbly black metal chairs.

Me with my blueberry bagel,
José with his cinnamon raisin,
and Mom with her messy everything bagel.

It was on a Sunday
and we didn't go to church.
We haven't gone to church
for months now.

I wonder if we ever will again.

I wanted to ask
how Mom can feel Catholic
without going to church
but I didn't want to upset her.

Instead I told her and José
I was working on a new comic
with my friend Ryan.

Mom said, "I didn't know you still did comics."

I told her about
my favorite graphic novels
and about how I want to write one someday.

They seemed actually interested.

I felt good.
Sometimes, my art
is like a bridge to my mom.

She understands it
and always tells me
how talented I am.

We wiped cream cheese
from our mouths
and sat together
and I thought that

things might be slowly
getting better.

WATCHING ESPN

There've also been a few nights
I've tried to watch the sports channel with Dad.

Even though at school I feel super comfortable in my gender,
at home I still feel like I'm proving myself,

especially to Dad.
I just never know what he's thinking, so sometimes

I like assume he's mad at me.
I wonder if he will ever see me as a son.

I guess I hope watching
BORING baseball games might help.

Half the time I don't know what's going on.
I want to ask him, "Why was that a strike?"

or "How come the batter just tapped the ball?"
but I try to google it instead, so I can like prove

I know things. Our team is the Yankees. It always has been.
One day I asked Dad, "Why do you like the Yankees?"

He turned to look at me.
"We're Yankees people. They're the best team."

"Oh . . . okay," I said,
kind of confused actually.

Then Dad said, "My dad and I used to go once a year.
Waiting in line to get into the stadium, he

would put me on his shoulders
so I could look out at everyone around.

I loved those games.
They're a part of me."

I thought a little bit about
how sports are like the only way cis straight guys

are like "allowed" to show emotions.
Still I asked, "Maybe if you have time
we could we go one day?
It's okay if not."

Dad put his hand on my knee.
"This summer all of us can go! Me, you, and José."

And I felt so so good.
Then he said, "My son and my daughter

at a Yankees game.
It'll be great."

And that one word,
daughter,

was like a knife in my heart.
I brushed it off

and kept watching the game with him.

ART SCHOOL

The only school that even
got back to me with a real answer
was NYU and they said "NO WAY!"
Well, actually they said
UNFORTUNATELY and
then I didn't read the rest because
we all know what
UNFORTUNATELY means.
I didn't tell you this, Oliver, because you were
so happy that YOU got into NYU
and
I don't want to kill your hype about it.
I keep wondering
what I could have done different.
I keep wondering
if maybe I'd gone to my new school longer
if maybe I'd taken more art classes
and been a better artist.
I know it sounds like bragging
but at Kutztown I was just always the best.
I won all the art competitions
and was in all the art classes.
Here, it's like everyone's so good!
They push me to want to keep getting better
but I feel kind of behind.
And, man, it's going to suck
if none of the schools I applied to work out.

I just thought
I was sure to get into at least one of them
and now I'm not so sure.
Will you still like me if
I'm not going to school like you?
Will you still get me
like you do now?

WAIT LIST

What I mean by "real" answer
is all these other schools
put me on the wait list

which is a terrible place
equal to the purgatory
of college acceptance.

Does that make rejection hell?

Maybe.

Maybe that's

an exaggeration.

I mean, José didn't go to college right after high school
and he's amazing.

I guess what's worse
than the fact that they didn't like my art
enough to accept me

is that they just leave you waiting.

I feel like graduation should
be the end of a chapter

but I'm so uncertain about
what's going to happen.

I feel like I'm in limbo

while I watch you
and my friends plan
for going away next fall.

I wish I had more help or at least
someone to give me more options.

I know I should have applied more places
but I didn't even know
I could ask to have the application fees waived
till last week when my art teacher asked
if I'd requested it.
What good is the help if no one
is there telling you about it?

I just feel like
the whole thing isn't fair.

Do I even want to go
to art school?

I could just be an artist
and not worry
about all the loans
and the stress.

Some of the best artists
never went to art school.

Ugh, I don't know
what to do anymore.

FOREVER A KUTZTOWNIAN

In the last few months
my whole world has like
exploded.

There are so many places
I want to show you
in the city.

My favorite so far
is Battery Park.
It's a pretty long subway ride away

from where I live
in Jamaica, Queens.
What's funny about New York

is that every neighborhood
is like a different town.
Like, from where I'm living

Forest Hills feels like
as far as Fleetwood is from Kutztown.
But instead of driving through cornfields

you take a subway ride.
Does that make sense?
Maybe not.

I've noticed tourists also seem to think
I'm from here. Maybe it's because
of my brown skin?

I don't know.
But I'm always like,
"I'm sorry, I would be totally lost

if it weren't for the wonders of
Google Maps."
I still use my phone

to get like everywhere.
Whether I like it or not,

I think I'm always going to be
a Kutztownian
no matter how long I live here.

WHEN PRATT'S FINE ARTS DEPARTMENT ASKED FOR MORE OF MY WORK, I SENT THEM . . .

[Image of a dove.
The dove is standing in the fragments
of a shattered stained-glass window.]

[Image of the host,
a priest holding the bread up.
There's a target painted
on the host.]

[Image of two boys standing
in front of a grave. They are holding
hands and they are kissing.]

VOICE MAIL

You (Oliver):

AHHHHHH
you're graduating, can you believe that?

I'm graduating tomorrow,
can you believe that?

I don't know what else to tell you
but we made it
        can you believe that?

And we're like both going to
be in the city together next year
        can you believe that?

Text me—I'm thinking
about you!

You're killing it!

Love you so so so so much!

BATHROOM

I hold the phone close to my head
to listen to your voice mail
in the big stall of the boys' bathroom

with my graduation robes on.

We'll have to line up
in a few minutes.

I always use the big stall because
it's the only place
I feel like I have enough space
and sometimes I'm scared

people will tell me to
use the other bathroom
or yell at me

or worse.

No one ever has said anything
and I feel lucky because

my friend Frankie who's
a trans girl had to hide
in the big stall once because
boys were teasing her.

She was using the boys' room
because she was scared to use
the girls' room.
I told her I would go with her
to any bathroom she wanted.

It's such a simple thing
and I think it's so stupid it's the only freaking thing
people ever talk about with trans people as if
all we think about is wanting to use the bathroom.

I'm sitting here feeling so down
while everyone else is excited
about graduation.

Your voice mail reminds me
that I lied to you in April and told you I got
into Pratt and into the New School.

You had just gotten accepted
to all your schools
and I wanted to give you
some good news for once.

HOW DO YOU TELL YOUR BOYFRIEND?

College isn't the same
for me.

Not that college isn't hard
to get into in general,

but for me, art school
just feels so personal right now.

The papers you submitted
for your applications
were personal, I'm sure

but not in the same way
my canvases are.

When I took pictures of each
piece to send them away
for someone else to judge

I felt like I was sending
children away to war.

There were a few drawings
that I sent you
that I just couldn't
bring myself to send
to an art school.

They were too real.

Sometimes when I paint
the canvas I pretend
the big blank square
is my own back.

I don't tell you this;
I don't want you to think
that I'm not proud of you.

I'm so proud of you.

When do you tell your best friend/
boyfriend that you're
not going to school together

in the city next year?

That you don't know
what you're doing

at all?

"WHERE ARE YOU GOING NEXT YEAR?"

If one more person asks
me that this week I'm going to die.

My parents have resorted
to phrasing the question
in all sorts of new ways.

"Where do you think
you'll be in the fall?"

"Will you be able
to eat as an artist?"

"Haven't you always
wanted to be a doctor?
A nurse? You see how that worked
for us. It's practical.
We can always find jobs.
You can do that while you see
where the comic books take you."

"Haven't you always wanted
to be a professor?"

"Haven't you always
wanted to fix pipes like *Tío*
or teach high school like Nina?
Those are steady jobs."

Their expectations kind
of drop each time they ask.

I wonder if they'll ask
me to move out.

Probably not,
at least not right away.

While I'm here they
can pretend there isn't this chasm

between us right now.

I usually just reply,
"Maybe.
Maybe.
Maybe."
Hoping someone else
will change the subject.

I wish they'd ask me,
"What makes you happy?"

"What do you imagine?"

"How can we help you get there?"

BEING A GIRL/BOY

I've stopped correcting my parents
about my name and pronouns.

Well, actually, I guess I was
never too loud about it in the first place.

I'm still scared that if I speak up for myself too much
they'll just completely
push me away.

On the other hand
maybe they're waiting for me to lead—

I just wish it were easier.

After I first came out

sometimes I'd say,
calmly and patiently,

"I like the name Aaron, actually,"

after they called me [****]

but they'd just keep calling me
[****].

Once, José asked,
"Can I correct them?"

and I wanted him to
but it still felt weird
so I told him, "No."

After graduation
Mom asks, "Can we take you
out to eat?"

There's this fancy restaurant
a block from school
that all my other friends

are going to but
I tell Mom and Dad that I don't
want to go there.

I don't want them around
my friends who will call me
the right name
and the right pronouns.

So, instead, I tell Mom and Dad
I want to go to the little diner
two blocks over.

I get hit with this intense
fiery desire for you to be there
with me.

You're the only person
who can call me
by my other name
around my parents
and it might not sound so wrong.

It's like you're the bridge
between the person I am now
and the person I was in Kutztown.

FROOT LOOPS

I order Froot Loops
and my mom says,
"Baby, you know you can
get anything, right?"

I say, "Yes,"
and I still order the
Froot Loops.

The waiter brings them
in a miniature box.

I don't think I've ever
eaten Froot Loops
and been disappointed.

I mostly wanted to
remember
the mornings

in middle school when
you would bring them
as a snack
to homeroom
and I would

eat raisin bran
and you'd tease me playfully
and say it was
an "old person" cereal.

I don't tell anyone this
but I think of you
shaking handfuls
of the sugary Os into our hands
and pouring them into your mouth.

Oh, Oliver,
I wish you could be here.

GRADUATION NIGHT

We all come home
and flop down
on our frumpy green-gray sofa.

Dad says
"[****], I'm proud of you.
How do you feel?"

"All right," I say,
and I almost tell him
how much him calling me [****] affects me—

how it has the power
to suck the light and the joy
out of even a night
as exciting as this.

"Oh, come on, be excited," Mom says,
and she hugs me and kisses
my forehead.

I'm sandwiched between them
on the couch.

I share a look with José,
who sits on the folding chair
across the room,
and I feel a little better knowing
he sees how hard this can be for me.

I remind myself
that I only came out
a few months ago.

I know it might take some time.
It might take some time.
It might take some time.

But I am here right now
and my life is happening right now.

"I am excited," I say to Mom.
I smile slightly.

"You're free from high school!" José says.
"How does it feel?"

"It feels . . . not real yet.
I think I have to like let it sink in awhile," I say.

Mom asks, "Did your friends in Kutztown
have their graduation yet?"

I think about you
and the blue curtain in the auditorium
and all the people I used to know

lined up
without me.

Do you think of me?

Does anyone else think of me?

"They didn't yet—it'll be tomorrow," I say.

"Well, that'll be nice for them,"
Mom says before flicking
the TV on.

3:43 A.M.

Phone ringing

You (Oliver): Ugh, ah, hello?

Me (Aaron):
whispering
Hi!

You (Oliver): Aaron?

Oh, hi! Aw, hey

Your voice sounds different.

Me (Aaron): How so?

You (Oliver): I don't know.
I haven't heard it in so long.

We should have called each other sooner.

Me (Aaron): I should have.

You (Oliver): Are you okay?

Me (Aaron): I don't know. I think so.
I just wanted to hear you.

You (Oliver): Well, I'm here!

Me (Aaron): I graduated . . . you graduate
tomorrow? Right?

You (Oliver): Yeah! We're going to
go out afterward.

I wish you could come.

Me (Aaron): I do, too.

You (Oliver): I think about you.

Me (Aaron): I think about you, too.

You (Oliver): Why did you call now?

Me (Aaron): I didn't want to go to sleep without calling you.

You (Oliver): I saw on Instagram that you won
the award for art at your high school,

Guess who won ours here?

Me (Aaron): Was it Lizzy Huntz?

You (Oliver): No! They gave it to Janet Hall.
And Lizzy was pissed.

Me (Aaron): That's so funny. Last
I checked she only painted trees.

You (Oliver): Yep, that's about it.

Me (Aaron): I'll let you sleep now.

You (Oliver): Okay. I love you.

Aaron: I'm sorry that I never say
it back.

You (Oliver): It's okay.

I get it. It's kinda weird

when we're not together.

Me (Aaron): Next weekend, right?

You (Oliver): Less than a week away!
Did you talk to José about letting us
use his Uber app?

Me (Aaron): Yeah! I did. He said
I should have just told my mom but there's no way
she'd have let me go.
He's just always so optimistic about
stuff like that.
But yeah, he said it was fine
and it could be my graduation present.

You (Oliver): It's gonna be a pretty huge Uber bill . . .

Me (Aaron): I feel bad.
We could pay José back?

You (Oliver): I'm sure José would tell you if he couldn't pay for it

Me (Aaron) : You're right. I'm just not used to
doing stuff for like myself, you know?

You (Oliver): You deserve it, Aaron.

Me (Aaron): I hope I didn't grow too much.

You (Oliver): The uniforms aren't too tight
so it should be fine.

You're going to look so spiffy!

Me (Aaron): *Spiffy* isn't what I usually aim for,
but sure ... sure, I'll be ... well-dressed.

You (Oliver): I'm sorry. I'm a dork, aren't I.

Me (Aaron): Oh my God ... yeah,
but I wouldn't do anything fun without you.

You make me try stuff I wouldn't.

It's honestly sad that liking something a lot would make
you a dork just 'cause it's history and not
video games or something.

You (Oliver): Aw, you get me.
I'm gonna cry.

Me (Aaron): Noooo.

You (Oliver): I'm trailing off on ya here, love ...
I'm sorry.

We'll be together soon!

Me (Aaron): Oh! I'm sorry, go to bed! Get some rest.

You (Oliver): Good night!

QUESTIONING

Mom: So, what friends will you be with?

Aaron: Ryan, Gloria, Jackson, Marzio.

Mom: Why are you so quiet?

Aaron: I'm just thinking.

Mom: Where are you staying?

Aaron: Wildwood.

Mom: Where? Address?

Aaron: 334 Shore Breeze Way.

Mom: When are you getting there?

Aaron: Around noon tomorrow.

Mom: Give me your ETA when you leave in the morning.

Aaron: Okay.

Mom: Why are you so quiet?

Aaron: I'm being interrogated.

Mom: Okay. Send me updates.

Aaron: Mom!

Mom: Don't "Mom" me—I can stop you
from going at any time.

Aaron: I love you, Mom.

Mom: I'll keeping asking
as much as I want.

DID YOU TALK ME INTO THIS?

A part of me
feels really bad
about lying
and scared
that something
will go wrong
and I'll need
to call Mom and Dad
and I'll have
to explain that
I lied and
then they'll be
DISAPPOINTED
which is the worst
of all things.
I don't even
know where Monmouth is.
This was a terrible
idea why would
you talk me
into this
or did I talk
you into this?
I don't know
anymore but
I also have this
terrible worry
that I'll figure
out I don't
click with you anymore
or like you like THAT

anymore and
it'll be awkward
and terrible
and we're going
tomorrow and
I check my email
eighteen times in one hour
hoping to hear I got
accepted somewhere.
The alarm goes off
at seven a.m.
I grab my red backpack.
I'm meeting you
at the bus station in
Kutztown where we used
to sometimes sit and watch
the buses coming and going,
trying to guess where each passenger
was headed.
After I get there, we'll
get an Uber to
Monmouth, which
might just be the most expensive
Uber ever but I got graduation
money so I should be able
to pay José back,
though shouldn't I be saving
that for school?
And oh God I've
never even been somewhere
without my parents—
God how fucking lame—
it's not even that far I'm

just worried something
dumb will happen
or we won't like each other
or we'll get separated
or lost or
or
or
or

SEEING YOU

I didn't say bye to Mom when I left
so I know I'll get a text
later and she'll threaten to come get me
which . . . would be so freaking dramatic of her.

Ha-ha . . . she would do that too.
She'd drive all the way to the beach just to find me
not there.

I bet she'd interrogate
my friends until they confessed.

I do love my mom
so much.

I have this dream
that someday she'll defend me
as a trans boy to all our relatives
and all our family members
and the church
and her friends.

It *is* kind of funny to think of her
marching onto the battlefield pushing down

dudes dressed as soldiers to yank me
off the field by the collar
of my uniform.

So I'm thinking about Mom
on the whole bus ride to Kutztown,
but then

I almost start crying
when I start to recognize landmarks:

The old defunct water park between
two vineyards.

The ice cream place
with the giant soft-serve sculpture
on the side of 222.

When I finally get in, I decide to start
walking toward your house
and I'm feeling bad about
lying to Mom and then

there you are

at the bus stop.

You're not looking
at me; your eyes
wander aimlessly up the street,
scanning the rooftops and then
the hill with
the huge cemetery
we used to walk through together.

You have a rolling suitcase.
I remember seeing it once

tucked in the rack
above your dresser.

All the sensations fill me:
Sweet cucumber-melon hand lotion.
Your black hoodie, elbows worn down.
Pancakes and syrup floating up to your bedroom.
The sound of your bare feet on the stairs in the morning.

"Oliver," I say loud
without meaning to.

You perk up
and smile.

OLIVER

Oliver Oliver Oliver
Oliver Oliver
Oliver

is such a beautiful boy
who I love
who is kind
who is wonderful

who is breathtaking

and damn it

Oliver Oliver Oliver

Oliver Oliver

I'm such a mess.

I'm such a mess.

I'm crazy.

I'm ridiculous.

Oliver.

ON NORTH WHITE OAK STREET

"Oliver!" I shout,
and now you see me

and you start waving your arms

like you're going to
take off.

A bird, I think,
that's beautiful
and funny
and kind of ridiculous.

I don't know if I'm laughing
or crying or screaming

and are people looking at us?
Of course not,
it's early and
there's barely anyone around.

I'm hugging you and
you smell the same

as you did before

and for some reason
more than anything
else I'm happy

that you smell the same.

You feel the same
too, like one of those
super soft blankets,

the gray one on your bunk bed.

"I can't believe it's you!"
you say.

Nothing else exists
but us.

I want to kiss you
all over

I want to be
in your room

before your parents
knew anything

before we knew
anything

when we lay next
to each other,

opened the window,

and let our
names go.

SO FAST

I want to say
everything at once,

open my mouth:

tell you about
the art class in my new school which
is also the school I just graduated from which is
also not even my school, then, I guess. I want to tell
you about how me and José are talking, finally talking
again, and how each day I feel like our family might get better
and they might have enough room to want to learn
about me and
accept me and how happy I am for you
that you committed to NYU
and how I hope you teach history one day
and how before I left I was
working on paintings
of the creek behind our house, our old house, I guess.

Instead I can't say
anything, not at first. We just hold each other,
waiting for a driver to accept our trip
which takes forever and I'm worried
one will never come

and we'll miss the whole battle
and you'll be disappointed
and I try to google a bus that might
get us close but you tell me
to calm down and just
enjoy being back in town.

You start running through a checklist
of everything we'll need the next few days
and I wonder if you're doing it
because you're scared to talk to me.

UNIFORMS CHECKLIST

Shoes—
2 pairs
both brown
with shiny buckles

Gaiters—
2 pairs
that go around
the ankles

Cravats—
2
like soft,
light scarves

Tricornered hats—
2
which we remove from our
bags and put on
as we wait for the Uber

as if we're wading into
the past

as if the ride
is a time machine
taking us home.

Frock coats—
2
with brass buttons
across the chest in two
neat rows

The uniforms
are more formal
than a freaking prom tuxedo
and a part of me loves this
because I never went
to a prom and

I feel guilty about
not trying to take you.

Knickers—
2
which is just a dumb way
of saying pants

but I'm following your list
and I do like to sound historical
and all.

Fife—
just 1
and it's yours and

you never told me you
taught yourself to play
just for this trip.

You show me
the wooden instrument
and play a trill of notes

which almost sounds
like the birds
in the nearby trees.

TOO LATE

I grab your wrist too tight

as we sit down in the back
of the Uber.

The man is older than

I thought Uber drivers usually are.

But then again, I'm used to
taking rides in the city with José.

We take Uber or Lyft all the time because
José hates the subway.
I tried to tell him
that it's easy and fun
but José was like, "I know I know,
but I just always have this fear
that it'll get stuck underground."

After he said that
every time I took the subway
I would picture the tunnel
closing around us.

I'd start to think about
how many trans people took the subway
each day through the city
and then I'd start to think about
history
and all the unknown lives
of trans people in the city.

It's like there's all this
swallowed knowledge
around us everywhere.

You know, there could have been
trans people in Kutztown
decades and decades before us
and even now.

KEITH HARING

There is a famous queer artist from Kutztown
named Keith Haring.

I didn't learn he was gay
till we had a lesson on him and "pop art"

at my new school.
Like, I knew about Keith Haring—

his bubbly jittery figures
are all over Kutztown.

I always liked his art.
I wish someone had told me

he was queer when I lived in Kutztown.
It might have reminded me

I'm not the first
or the last queer boy

to grow up in a tiny town.
We pass the park on the way out of town

where Keith Haring's
huge red dancing dog statue stands.

I want to tell you this
but then I think

you probably already know about him.
You always know more about history

than me . . . which is fine
but sometimes

like now
I want to tell YOU things

but I stop myself.
Why do I do that?

OUR UBER DRIVER

has bright brown eyes
and brown skin.
A rosary dangles
from his rearview mirror.
He reminds me of my grandfather
who I've only seen a few times.

I didn't think we'd end up here

and everything keeps hitting

me in waves.

Graduation Oliver Mom Dad
José Oliver Aaron Soldiers War
Gravestone Battle College
School Pancakes Father
Angels God Oliver Travel

"Are you tired?" you ask.

"No, I'm really scared," I say.

You sigh, "I am too . . . was this stupid?"

You laugh nervously.

"How much money do you have?" I ask.

You grin and reach into your wallet

to reveal a few twenties.

"Graduation money," you say, and wink.

I feel so goddamn lucky that

you think of everything.

We're still quiet as we leave Kutztown behind
and I'm feeling pretty freaking sad that
I only got a few minutes there.

I hadn't realized just how freaking much
I missed that place.

I thought I hated it there but really
I just hated feeling alone—
hated feeling like
I had nowhere to be totally myself.

I love the creek and the woods and even
the little shops of Main Street.

The more we sit in silence the more

I fill with the knowledge

that it's too late to go back,

not just from the ride but

from everything. I can't go back

to pretending to be a girl. I can't

go back to high school or to my old house

to draw the creek or to just being friends

with Oliver or to having no name at all.

I wipe a tear off with the back

of my hand.

NOT CRYING

"Are you okay?" you ask.

"We haven't talked like at all and I'm worried
I'm doing something wrong. What are you
thinking about?"

I'm embarrassed because
I always hate talking and pretending like
the Uber driver isn't even there.

"I just,
it's just so much all at once."

You take my head in your hands
and kiss my forehead.

"I know."

"I can't believe
we're just doing this."

"We are adults, Aaron."

"I know, I just, wow."

We laugh.

"Hey, I love you."

I want to say, "I love you too"

but I just give in
to the throbbing
behind my eyes and start
crying.

"It's okay, it's okay."

"I'm not crying," I say,
and then laugh, the tears
dropping on my lap.

OUR DRIVER'S NAME IS LAURENCE

and he says,
"You mind if I butt in?"

I feel kinda nervous.

What if he's some homophobic dude?

I wish I had just kept still instead
of getting all freaking emotional.

"Yes?" I say reluctantly.

"Growing up is hard," he says.

We both nod.

"You look like nice boys.
Now what are you up to?
I'm not going to rat you out
to anyone."

You seem excited to tell him
so I let you take the lead.

"We're going to a Revolutionary War
reenactment."

"Wow, that is . . . not what I expected."
He laughs. "Ha! I thought
you kids were running away."

I wouldn't mind running away.
I feel like I want to run away right now.

"I used to reenact, you know."

"Wow, really?" you ask.

"Yeah, I reenacted World War Two.
I'd pretend to be my dad.
He died when I was younger so
it made me feel connected to him, you know?"

"Wow, that's really powerful," you say,
and I'm envious of how good you are
at just dropping into conversations like this.

You bring the most freaking incredible stories
out of people.

THE TUSKEGEE AIRMEN

Laurence tells us about how his dad was
one of the Tuskegee Airmen,

which sounds like something
we might have talked about

in history class and now I feel kinda bad
that I didn't pay more attention.

He tells us about how
they were the first team
of Black military aviators—

fighter pilots.

His face lights up as he talks about
his father and how
even though he passed away
when Laurence was only in middle school,
knowing that his dad was part of that team
made him feel like he still knew him somehow.

He told us about how his mom thought
it would be strange to dress up as his dad
but when she came with him
to a World War II weekend show
and saw all the kids coming up
to ask him questions

she understood.

He says he stopped doing it
because he didn't feel like traveling
as much anymore but that his son
still reenacts.

It makes me think about
how much more I would like history class
if we talked more about queer people
and people of color
and people with disabilities
and people with different religious backgrounds
instead of just teaching about them
as side facts in a white guy's history.
What would a class about
the Revolution look like
thinking about those groups?

Then again,
I'm no historian.

It seems like that would take
a whole lot of work.

Oliver, I hope
you teach high school history someday
because I bet I would love your class.

THE VIEW

While we chat

I look out the window and watch

the clouds and herds of mist ribboning

between trees in the mountains

we're driving though.

It all feels like science fiction, like

we're in a time machine,

like maybe during this trip

nothing that's real has to be real,

like I can pretend we're going back to 1778

for good and I'll never have

to go home and explain to my family

where I was.

I know I wouldn't have fit in

back then and I'm so grateful for so much

but imagining the escape makes me feel like

I have options—

like I'm not trapped in the life

we're living.

Sometimes I think

I'm in the wrong timeline—

like in another universe

there's a boy named Aaron who has things

so much easier.

He's still trans, yes, but his parents are so supportive

and he never had to move and he doesn't have

to sneak away for the weekend.

You would miss your family,

I know.

Would I grow to miss

my own?

YOUR HAND

You fall asleep pretty early on
in the drive and I think
about waking you up.

In a lull in the conversation
you just kind of drift off.

"Looks like we lost your friend,"
Laurence jokes.

I don't want to be alone
with all my thoughts.

I want to text my mom
but I'm scared of
giving us away.

I wonder about the names of
the rivers
and the creeks we pass.

Your hand is open
on your lap, almost
like you're in some kind
of yoga position.

I touch your hand lightly,
just to check again that
this is all really happening.

Your skin is a little sweaty,
which makes me smile
because whenever we held
hands you would stop
to wipe your palms on
the front of your pants.

TALKING TO LAURENCE

I decide to try to make some small talk.
Ha-ha . . . following in your footsteps.
I say, "Do you know
who Keith Haring was?"

Laurence furrows his brow.
I watch his face in the mirror.
"Is he the guy who makes
those little cartoon guys all over town?"

"Yeah!" I say. "Do you live in town
or nearby?"

"I've lived in town my whole life.
We used to have a little farm but
now I'm old and don't feel like dealing with that.
Do you like Keith Haring's art?"

"Yeah I do. I do a lot.
Did you know he was gay?"

Laurence smiles. "I did know that
but I hadn't thought about it for a while.
That's important. It's important to remember
all the aspects of people we admire."

"It is, I think it is," I say
and I feel kind of accomplished.
I think I've leveled-up in small-talk skills
just on this Uber ride.

WHAT HISTORY

I have a funny thought
about us and that
we're in a history book
right between all sorts
of important stuff
like wars and biplanes
and machine guns.
Right in the middle of all
that stuff is a picture
of you asleep on a drive
to New Jersey, your soft features
even brighter in the glint
of the sun through the window.

The mini unit would
be just about two trans boys
who grew up to be trans men
who lived and loved each
other in a small town
in rural Pennsylvania.
Nothing about my family
or college or anything,
just about us on
this trip.
Young trans kids
would read it and love
us even if we weren't
in a war or doing anything
heroic. I think about
that a lot, though, how
our soldiers probably
didn't want to go to war.
I would love them
even if they hadn't been soldiers,
if they had just been lovers
who hid away in the mountains.
Why do our stories always
have to be ones
of suffering and longing?
I want to end happy
with you.

TWO HOURS

can be a whole lifetime.

At first, I thought about the journey
all fantastically, like me and you would

live on the road, but
it's been about two hours now and
all that is gone.

I want to wake you up now
and talk like we used to
in hushed voices
under covers.

I nudge your shoulder
and you press your head
against the window.

"Wake up, Oliver,"
I say frantically, the anxiety
spilling out of me.

"What, what?" you ask,
grabbing my arm.
"Is something wrong?"

"Oh . . . no, I just got lonely."

You grin and take
my hand

and then we're both embarrassed
because Laurence is pretending
to look away.

I feel bad he has to drive us.
Even though we're paying I always
feel weird having things done for me.

"Can we talk?" I ask.
"I'm nervous 'cause we're almost there."

"Of course, what
should we talk about?"

GODDAMN IT

I start crying?

Like what?

Oliver's usually the guy
always crying.

I didn't even cry when I left!

I'm covering
my face with my hands.

Twice in one day?

Is it still the same day?

Who knows.

I JUST RAMBLE

Start telling him everything.
I go from little details to big ones.

I tell him about
the way
the hallways smelled different
in my new/old school

and how each day I wondered
whether or not it was just
because I was used to his smell
wherever we went.

I tell him about
how I wish my family
accepted me totally and completely and how
I'm fucking sick

of pretending like
it doesn't get to me
every single day.

I tell him about
purposefully not saying
"I love you" back
because I feel like
I can't go back after that.

OLIVER SAYS

"It's okay if you don't say it.
It's okay if you never can.

I used to be upset that you don't
and sometimes it still makes me sad
but I wouldn't want you to say it
unless you meant it.

It's okay,

it's okay."

GO BACK

"Do you think you can take us back?"
you ask Laurence,
and he looks at me.

"Do you not want to go?" I ask.

"No, I'm just scared,
like what if our parents freak out?"

"How would they even know, Oliver?
It's going to be okay.
Let's just keep going."

Laurence adds, "It's scary
but if I found out my boy went on a trip
to a reenactment I can't imagine being
that upset with him."

"I don't know," you say.

There start to be signs for
the reenactment.

They feature rows of militiamen
with their weapons ready
and smoke blooming around them.

I imagine for a moment
that this is a time machine

and that we've actually gone back
to the 1700s.

Would we have heard
the sound of war
in the distance?

What did war sound
like back then?

Drums? Marching? Yells?

I'm worried.
I wish I was braver, like real people in real history.

I feel small.

LAURENCE

We say our goodbyes
to Laurence and he
writes his email on a napkin from
his glove box.

He tells us to email him
about how the reenactment goes
and he'll send us some pictures
of his uniform if we want.

He says we should stay close together
and be careful
and we tell him we will.

He says that
his son is just like us,
which catches me off guard.

I go through a list of things
that we are—
eighteen, reenactors,
short, brown-haired—

and then I realize as
Laurence nods
that he means
trans
and I wish

we could have talked longer
and I think about

what you said about how
there's a million trans people

in the United States

and I think of them like

stars glittering
across the map.

ENTRANCE

I haven't been on a real trip for
what feels like
forever.

Moving to New York
kinda felt like
almost a whole school year of vacation
but a stressful vacation.

My family hasn't gone anywhere
for a few years at least.

The last trip we took was to
Baltimore, but José and Dad argued
half the time and the sharks
at the aquarium were asleep, so
I was pretty pissed off.

I was too little
to remember

when we all went to Puerto Rico
to see family.

My parents always talk
about it like I should
know all the details.
José, too.

José was older but
he doesn't remember it either.

He told me one afternoon
when we were alone together
that he practiced the stories
he had about Puerto Rico
so that when our parents brought
it up he would have something
to say.

"Sometimes I don't
feel Puerto Rican," he said.

"Me either," I said.

Which wasn't totally true.
There are things that still
make me feel Puerto Rican
It's just complicated sometimes.

Walking up to the entrance
of the reenactment
and festival
I wish I'd picked
a more "Puerto Rican" name.

I feel like it might make
it easier for my parents
to accept me but

not just for them.

I feel like it might
make me feel more whole.

I don't know.

Maybe I'm just trying to find
a solution to all the feelings
whirling inside me.

Would you understand?

Can you change your name
more than once?

BACK IN TIME

There are no real bathrooms,
so we go to the porta-potties at the edge
of parking lot

to change into our uniforms.

It's tight in there
with both of us in one room.

We help each other
into all the button-up pieces
and strange-fitting clothes.

"We're going back in time,"
you say,
looking at me in uniform
in the gross dim light
coming into the bathroom.

"Some time machine,"
I joke.

FESTIVAL

I'm thinking about
choosing a different name

than Aaron
as we navigate the different tents
full of craftspeople and food.

We're like goldfish
in a huge rushing creek.

People of all ages
meander from booth to booth.

There's light music
playing and I wish
I were better at dancing because
it makes me want to.

There are a few picnic benches
in front of a food vendor,
so we plop down there.

I'm laughing
as I read the menu.

"What?" you ask.

"Hamburgers and fries," I say,
setting my bag down in the grass
underneath our table.

"You think they had hamburgers
in the Revolutionary War?" you ask.

The familiar smell of fries
and sound of sizzling grease
are comforting.

"Do you want to eat here?" you ask.

"I wanted to get something like
'authentic' or whatever but

it smells too good.
I think we should give in."

"Thank goodness,
I was thinking
the same thing,"
you say.

"We have all two days
to try something different."

WHILE EATING FRIES

"I don't think I have a home anymore," I say.

"What do you mean?"

"I can feel it like disappearing."

"Your home? Disappearing?"

"More like a *sense* of home, I guess," I say.

"You should be a philosophy major
and an art major," you say.

That strikes a chord and reminds me
I haven't told you that
I'm not really a major anywhere
or studying anywhere
because I'm not going anywhere.

I'm not going
anywhere anywhere anywhere.

"Right," I say.

"Are you mad?" you ask.
Which is what you say whenever
I try to hide something.

"No, just tired."
Which is what I say whenever
I don't want to talk about it.

I start to remember all
the times last summer
when this would make us argue.

We didn't argue a lot
but this was how it always started
when we did.

I hope we don't argue.

"That's understandable," you say.

"I hope I do okay
in the actual battle," I say.

"What do you mean?"

"I don't know, we're just so close to doing
everything we planned."

"We made it here," you say,
and you take my hand
and kiss it.
"It's gonna be okay."

OUTSIDE THE STATE PARK

Mountains like the fins of

great sharks great fish

flowers pouring like water soft bread clouds

piles of hay I'd like to climb on top of one

place pacing in fields I'd like to talk to some of them

ask their names   say my name is "Aaron"   and them answer

with a rustle of green and bird calls and ancient bark.

I roll my name around beneath my tongue. I zone out
and listen to

the commotion of the encampment. So many
costumes even children dressed up

I love how we turn words around in our mouths

The fields nearby are like straw-colored patches great
quilt great huge

so huge sky sky
purple sky blue sky sky sky

Would you blame me if I change

my name to Sky?

THE BRITISH

"Lads! Where do you come from!"
a man sitting at the table beside ours asks.

I'm so surprised
that everyone sees us as boys here!

At first I'm worried
and then it's thrilling.

I wonder if I could get away with
dressing like this every day.

Ha—no, I don't mean that,
but it's definitely awesome.

The guy is really nice and
he says he's always excited to see

young people participating in history.

You stay in character and say,
"We shouldn't be fraternizing
with the Brits but
thanks so much for saying hello.
This is our first time."

"Well, you have to go to the dance Sunday.
You do know about the dance, right?"

"We didn't!"

"It's just in the barn over there.
It'll be nice,
and plenty of young ladies,"
he says, winking.

It all seems too easy.

Too smooth.

I hold your hand

without meaning to
and the guy doesn't notice.

I pray.

PRAYING

I hate it.
I don't want to pray.

I avoid praying at all costs most of the time.

My mom is the one who prays before dinner.
She's kept praying
even though it makes José upset

and she'd say,
"*Mijo*! We need to pray. We have to keep praying.
They win when we stop praying,
when we give up hope."

I still don't know what she
means by *they* or what she has *hope* for.

People who don't believe in God?
People who want us not to believe in God?
The sex-abuser priests?

I guess it's all different for me
because I stopped trusting priests
a long time ago.

I was a freshman, maybe,
when I started to hate the homily
at church.

The priest talking
about the sin of masturbation.

I could still touch myself,
sure, but I'd have to think about him.

I hated that,
that what he said remained
somewhere deep inside me.

But looking out
around us

I pray in my head.

SANTA MARIA

Dios te salve, Maria,

I still prefer to pray to Mary
even though she's a woman
and I'm a man.

llena eres de gracia;

I don't know what to make of it
that I sometimes miss
things about being a girl.

El Señor es contigo.

I want to ask you if
you do, too.

I wonder if it will be different
if/when we take hormones.

*Bendita Tú eres entre todas las mujeres,
y bendito es el fruto de tu vientre,*

You are beautiful.
I'm picturing us
on the ride here again.

You roll down the window,
just a crack.

The air smells different here
but also the same.

Wet farmland.
Tilled earth.

Jesús.
Santa María, Madre de Dios,
ruega por nosotros, pecadores,

The words spin through
me again and again.

I want to ask if you
are praying, too.

ahora y en la hora de nuestra muerte.

What you pray for.

Do you pray for us?

Amén.

PATRON SAINT OF TRANS BOYS

Sometimes I think
if there was a trans saint
maybe I could teach my mom about them
and she'd understand
that queer people
are holy in our own ways.

I could have a way
to explain my manhood
to my dad.

I guess though
I don't even know if I care about
being holy.

When I say
there are things I miss
about being a girl

I think I really mean
I miss moving in the world
feeling seen at least
in some way.

TOY SET

This place looks
like a toy set

I saw once on your dresser where you had little

plastic soldiers red blue white

some on horseback and some with their rapiers drawn

I always wondered what you thought about as you arranged them

if you invented lives for your figures or if

you simply saw them for the plastic

they were.

A PAINTING

This place is like a painting
a history-book diagram

another life like we lived here before.

Like muscle memory.

Like we are living as ourselves again.

Like this was our life we are reenacting.

Do you think that's possible?

No reincarnation but maybe

that living people can have some sort of

connection to dead people?

Kind of like being Instagram followers.

Connected but not in bodies?

Am I making sense?

WHERE ARE WE?

The Revolution.

What revolution?   Whose revolution?

Ours

it could be ours.

Who are   *we?*

We young queer boys   we genderqueer   we gay

we bisexual we soft hands we gentle minds we lesbian

we transgender

we nonbinary we transcendent

we asexual we romantics we loving

we somehow adults

and we bodies

and fingers and knees and mouths

we thrive in any time

we want.
We could belong there.

UNDER AN OAK TREE

"I feel old," you say

as we spend the first hour or so
meandering around
the craft tents.

It's almost like
a whole village here and

the more conversations I hear in character,
the more I feel like we're drifting
away from who we were before.

"I do, too."

At the end of a row of tents we take a second
under a huge old oak tree

and I wonder if the tree's been there
since the actual Revolution.

You never know.
There are trees that old
and some even older.

IMPULSE

We both look at our phones while
we talk, trying
to connect to some Wi-Fi
from one of the nearby tents or cabins,
but we can't find any public networks.

"I'll make a hot spot," you say
which I think is dumb because
we don't really need internet but at the same time
I'm also feeling internet deprived.

Both our phones BING
and vibrate with messages.

"Mom?" you ask.

"Mom," I say, nodding and
scrolling.

MOM

I love you, be safe

Let me know when you get there

Haven't heard from you

Why do you have to worry me?

Text your brother if not me

When you get home you're never leaving again if
you don't check in with us

I'm sorry we're just worried

Did you get anything to eat?

Have you eaten enough?

You know we do love you

I know it's been hard

Love you so much baby

TAKE A PICTURE

I take
my hat off and
zoom the camera in close.

I position
the sun in the background
so it's blaring and bright behind me as if we're
out on the beach or a boardwalk.

I turn off the location so it doesn't show up.
I send the picture to Mom.

I feel guilty,
like I should keep trying
to talk to her.

Sometimes I make her out
to be this terrible person
when I know there have been so many changes
for her, too.

Me: I'm having fun!

Mom: You're okay?

You look good.

Are you eating?

Me: Duh Mom!
You know me
I'm always
hungry.
Sorry I forgot
to check my phone

Mom: Don't forget again 😈

AFTERNOON

After a few hours
anywhere can start to feel routine.

It kind of reminds me
of the first few nights
in the city—how I slowly but surely
found a pattern of my own.

We start to get used
to the air and the pulse
and to each other again.

I haven't been so close to you
in so long.

I feel so so much older here.

Like we're out of college,
like we have our own family,
maybe kids and a goldfish
and a dog

and this is where we go
on a trip together.

Usually you're the one
who thinks about stuff like that
in the future.

I feel bad for not
telling you
what I'm thinking.

I could live in 1778 for
much longer than a few days.

We could meander
and become blacksmiths or tavern keepers
or messengers or whatever they had
back then.

"We should find a spot
to set up our tent," you say.

I've been so dazed by it all
that I forgot we have to camp.

"Do you think some people
stay at hotels nearby?" I ask.

"They'd be cowards!" you joke.
"And honestly, they might not
make it to the first battle
of the morning."

"Ha—true!" I say.

I worry about
meeting other people.

I worry they won't be like us.

I'm sure there are reenactors here
who can't stand people like us.

Maybe I'm just being judgmental.

More than anything
I'm worried it will ruin this for you.

I love how vibrant
you are here.

I haven't seen you like
this for so long.

SURREAL

"Are you . . . are you feeling something here?" I ask.

"I think so . . . I think it's the kind of thing
that's going to take time for it to like sink in."

There's a silence and
I imagine you're also thinking
about the soldiers—

our soldiers who reunite here
in our story.

I wish I hadn't
asked you if you were feeling something.

It could ruin the magic
if we try too hard to feel something
fantastical.

This all doesn't feel
like it's really my life.

You're really here.

We really are our soldiers

and the summer night
is arriving
cool and blue around us.

UNDER THE STARS

We're staking out
our place in the camping area
and struggling to figure out
the tent gear you bought.

"You know this is the kind of tent
the generals would have?"
you say.

"Really?
What did the soldiers sleep in?"

"Just in a sleeping bag unless
it was winter like Valley Forge,
where there were cabins, or on other occasions
the soldiers would actually
stay in people's houses."

"Houses?"

"Yep!" you say.

"Wait . . . so they just slept under the stars, then?"

You beam. "Yeah . . . they would."

"Do you want to?" I ask.

"I actually do."

We fold the tent up and lay it next
to our backpacks and sleeping bags.

We lie down for a second
in our separate sleeping bags
as the music trickles over us from the band
across the way
and the sunset glows
orange and purple.

"I feel like we're hyping
it up to be something . . .
I don't know,
more grandiose than it's going to be."

And I'm confused
because usually you're
always excited about stuff like this.

You seem
anxious about the battle tomorrow
and that this won't be worth it.

You've been looking down
at your phone a lot.

I wonder if I'm doing something wrong.

All the hard parts are over.
We made it here.

We just get to become our soldiers
and enjoy being together.

I don't know why you
always have to do this,
when everything's going so well.

"Did you text your mom?"

You nod.

"I texted mine, too."

You smile. "Was she freaking out?"

"Of course."

BESIDE US

A field with dozens
of people lying out
just like us.

You beside me
Me beside you.

We set our backpacks
by our heads.

I didn't know how much
I liked privacy until now.

I feel like
everyone and everything
can see me.

It's dusk,
orange glow
across the grass and trees.

"What are your names?"
one of the girls
close by asks us
after she waves.

"Oliver!"

"Aaron," I say
with some hesitation.

She furrows her brow.
"How old are you?"

You tell the truth,
"Eighteen."

I feel like she's inspecting us,
trying to understand what gender
we are.

But I might also be paranoid
or crazy.

Maybe she's really trying
to see if this is our first time.

I can tell she wants to
ask more but she
just explains that she's
from Virginia and her . . . she pauses
before saying
her *girlfriend*
is from New Jersey, but now
she lives in Virginia with her.

They went to college
at Monmouth together, where

they went to a reenactment once
just for fun.

Now they're back
as authentic pottery makers and
they love American history.

She says she's excited
when new people
come to this event.

"I'm starting college in the fall," you say,
"and so is he! We're very excited.
I'd love to go to a reenactment
in Virginia someday,
maybe I'll take him with me."

I shift nervously.

God! I hate how I get
awkward like this.

I focus in the distance on
the glowing sun

as you two talk.

I swear I can see it setting,
tucking itself under covers.

I stop listening
and survey the place
and pretend we're our soldiers
meeting locals in town

before battle.

CERISE

Later, the sun sets
and most of the chatter
comes from tents where men
twice our age drink cases of
beer they brought in coolers.

You say in a whisper,
inching your sleeping bag
closer to mine,

"Let's take a walk."

So we do.

I feel like a ghost
in the dwindling light.

I feel like we died here once,
which I know is stupid and superstitious of me.

"Her name is Cerise
and her sleeping friend is Acacia,"
you say,
snapping me back to reality.

"Who?"

"The people next to us?"

"I'm sorry, I just kind of
zoned out.
It's been
a long day."

"Yeah, I think
I'm like loopy from not sleeping

last night,
that's probably why I could talk
to them. I never talk
to people just out of the blue.
Like that."

"Really? I always think of you
as the one
who's good at talking,"
I say.

We come back and lie
quietly for a while.

I get used to the sound
of your breathing
and the distant chatter
and muffled voices.

"You ever think that
maybe we're different people
depending on where we are?" I ask.

"Maybe," you say.

I hoped you would say
more about that.

I wonder if I'm a different person
than when you last saw me.

"*Cerise* means 'cherry,'" you say,
reading from your phone.

"I think maybe if my name
was that pretty I might not
have changed it," I joke.

You keep staring at the screen.
"And *Acacia* is a kind of tree
with yellow flowers . . .
I would be Acacia . . .
I think everyone should
pick their own names, you know?
Not just trans people."

"I don't know, sometimes
I wish my parents would have
picked my name . . . it makes me feel
lonely," I say.

AWAKE

I'm awake and all alone.

You fall asleep early,
which is funny because
you had so much energy just
a few hours earlier.

You said you wanted
to just rest your eyes a moment
and I heard your light breathing
mixing with someone's snoring
(Cerise?) nearby.

You drift beside me,
asleep and peaceful.

Maybe you're dreaming?

You a raft.

You an airplane.

You a cruise ship.

You a balloon.

You a leaf drifting down the creek.
I'm at the bottom of the creek,

looking up at us when we were girls.

Should I say it like that?

"When we were girls."

It feels true even though
I know most trans people aren't comfortable
with saying things like that.
I'm not sure yet
if I am.

I wish everyone was allowed
more room to be unsure.

Sometimes I wish I'd
waited longer to come out,
till I had everything sorted out.

I stare at the now dark sky.

"Hey,"
that girl we met,
Acacia, whispers.

ACACIA

"I'm up too," she says.

I roll over to see her.

She's looking at me:
brown luminous eyes,
freckles across the bridge of her nose.

She's only a few yards away.

Beside her Cerise sleeps heavy,
and yes, she is the one snoring.

"Let's go," she says,
slipping out of her sleeping bag.

She stands and
waves for me to come over

though I'm not sure
where we'll go.

WHO IS AN ARTIST?

"You're not really very old,
are you?" she asks.

"What?"

"You're like twelve, right?"

I furrow my brow. "I'm eighteen."

She smirks,
"All right."

"I'm well aware
I look like a middle schooler,"
I say, trying to deflect how
the joke kinda hurts.

It reminds me that
even when people gender me correctly
they might not see me as "fully" a man.

Am I even a *man?*
I guess *boy* still feels more accurate
but I guess it feels like
people think I'm "boy lite"
or something.

I don't hold it against Acacia.
I know she's just joking around.

We make our way to shop tents,
where only a few dim lanterns are lit.

She leads us to her and Cerise's tent,
where inside are
beautiful displays
of all sizes of clay pots and basins
and vases and cups.

"I studied art in school,"
she says.

"I teach during the school year
but the summers are the best because
I get to really be a potter
like I dreamed of being.
I know it's old-fashioned
but secretly, so am I."

"Why secretly?"

She shrugs, "I guess
a lot of people assume
that being queer is like

some new thing, so queer people
wouldn't be interested
in colonial America.
There were
definitely queer people back then.
I kind of hate that queer history is
seen as like separate from 'normal' history."

"Fair," I say.
"I like art, too. I'm kind of an artist.
I make cartoons
and paintings, though."
I'm feeling pretty proud of myself
for saying that. I almost never
talk about being an artist.

"That's awesome!
Don't say 'kind of.'
You're totally an artist.
I'd love to trade.
Maybe a vase for a cartoon?"

"I'd love that."

"It's funny—I always have
a hard time calling myself a sculptor
or a potter, too.
I always tell people
it's just a hobby even though it's
so much a part of me."

COSMIC BROWNIES

"I was born a girl," I say
kind of out of the blue

as Acacia roots through boxes under
the table that looks like
a makeshift register.

"I thought so," Acacia says.
"It would be rude of me to say that, though.
I guess what I mean is
I thought you were queer but I didn't
want to say anything . . .

I'm sorry. I'm saying that wrong."

"I'm a boy.
No, it's okay. I know
what you mean."

Acacia nods. "I get it.
I'm sorry.
I didn't mean to
prod you about it.
I was just excited
to find someone else
like us."

"Do you mind if I ask why
we're here?"

Acacia laughs.

"Oh! Ha-ha. It's my little tradition.
So, Cerise only ever eats
period-accurate food because
she's super into authenticity
soooo I feel bad eating my modern snacks
in front of her. Of course, she doesn't mind
but I do, so I always sneak a few for myself

and after meeting you guys I thought
it would be more fun to share them."

She removes a box of
Cosmic Brownies.

They taste like elementary school
and they're delightful.

We share each package we open
as she tells me more about
how she thinks lesbians existed
as awesome spinsters during the Revolution.

"Is that why you and Cerise come here?
Because that's why me and Oliver did—
we think about how
there might have been trans soldiers."

She claps, "OMG, that's totally possible!
You read the articles about female soldiers?"

"Yes! That's what we were thinking.
Sure some were women but
two, maybe more,
could have also been
trans men.
Just like me and Oliver!"

"I love that.
We should make a website
or something all about this."

"What?" I ask.

"Queer history—all the places
where we think people like us
might have existed."

"You think we could?"

"That's totally something Cerise would be into."

She bites down on her half
of another brownie.
"We can't tell her about this."
She winks.

I finish my piece of brownie.

"I'll say we took a walk."

We wipe our hands in the grass
and hug before

we go back to our places
in the field.

AUBADE FOR A BATTLEFIELD

Mouthful:
Glowing smoke:

Stars crawled:

Like pill bugs:
Made a sun:

Bright on your:

Pale skin:

I won't wake:
You up:
Just watch light:

Press your eyelids:

Open like:
Pocket watches:

I want to wake up:

Over:

And over:

In this:
Glimmer:

Bird wings:

Sweeping cloud:

I'm the first one up:

In all the world:

PICNIC BREAKFAST

On a blanket we
sit with Cerise and Acacia
to have breakfast.
We only packed granola bars,
so they share the traditional bread
Cerise made and some fresh eggs
they fry for us on a skillet.
They talk about how they didn't date
very long before they got married
and laugh about lesbian stereotypes
of "U-Hauling it."
"What does that mean?" I ask
and Acacia explains, "It's like you bring a U-Haul truck
to move in on the first date."
You say "We're dating"

and the girls say "aw" in unison.
"That's so sweet."
"You're cute together."
We talk about Acacia's idea
to start a website or a blog for queer people
to share their history queer-theories and
you adore the idea. You say you can't wait
to start designing the website.
I say I can do art for it and Cerise says
she already has post ideas.
There are lulls in the conversation
but we have a lot to say to each other
for people from different worlds.
I wonder how many people there
are like Cerise and Acacia who
I would enjoy the company of
if we shared this field far
away from our homes. I wish
I could meet more people like
this, without all the other stuff
getting in the way, like school,
and college, and parents
and hometowns and genders.
You stand up
when you finally get your
phone working again.
"Eight voice mails!" you say.

EIGHT VOICE MAILS

You hold your phone to your head,
plugging one ear.

When you're done listening
to all eight you give
us all the run-down.

1.

Your mom was worried she hadn't
heard from you.

2.

Your mom was worried
she hadn't heard from you
AND she called my friends
who ALSO didn't pick up.

3.

My friends picked up
and SUCK at being convincing,
they said we went away from
the group which OF COURSE
made your mom more worried.

4.

Your mom turned on Snapchat
and thought there was a glitch
that we're . . . not at the beach.

5.

Your mom called my friends again.

6.

Your mom thought we
might have been kidnapped and
told you to find a way of sending
a message.

7.

Your mom connected the dots.
She realized we snuck away somewhere.

8.

You're going to be in trouble
when you get home. She's still worried
but just wants you to call her.

"It seems like it could be worse," I say.

"Yeah, because it's not your family," you say,
more sharply than I've ever heard you
talk before.

Cerise and Acacia eat quietly.
I feel bad for them that we're
making it uncomfortable.

I'm not used to you being upset,
usually it's me.

I realize that I just assume
everything's easier for you,
which isn't always fair.

I don't really know
how to apologize for that.

Things are quiet
and Cerise says,
"Growing up is hard.
I'm sorry, guys."

Acacia adds, "Growing up queer
is hard.

We're here for you two."

YOUR FAMILY

I used to imagine that
one day your parents would
adopt me. Especially when
we were in middle school
and my dad wanted to escort
me to the sixth-grade dance

and HE DID
and I was so embarrassed.
You got to wear
a flapper dress,
dark eye makeup,
the works.

I didn't even want to wear
a dress but I was mad that
your parents didn't care
what you wore, they just
let you go.

"Do you remember
when my dad took me
to the sixth-grade dance?"
I ask after Cerise and
Acacia leave to go tend their stall.

You laugh. "What a date."

"I was really jealous
of you," I say.

I don't always say
what I'm thinking like this.

"You were? I looked awful,
that was my drag phase."

I say,
"No, I mean you just
seemed like you could
do what you wanted."

"Yeah, I mean kinda.
My mom texted me like
constantly. We took three hours
to get ready. Maybe I'm
exaggerating but it felt
like that long.
She jabbed me in the eye
with the eyeliner stick.
I guess I did have fun, though."

"Would you ever wear
makeup again, you think?"
I ask.

You shrug.
"Maybe."

"Will you be in trouble, you think?"

"Can we not talk about
that now?" you say.

So we don't.

We just watch the clouds.

MY DAD

After talking about that middle school dance
I'm thinking about Dad

as we lie and look at the clouds—
I'm imagining a conversation with him

where I tell him
he needs to call me Aaron
or not talk to me anymore ever again.

I've never confronted my dad
about anything like that.

I think I'm angry at him
for only wanting to protect me

when I was a girl.
He used to take me
everywhere in town.

How can he not see
that I need him more than ever?

Maybe I should start
by just telling him

I miss him.

How the hell
am I thinking about my dad

right now?!?!

WHEN GOING TO BATTLE

When going to battle
in a place that feels three hundred years ago
you have to expect to be lost and confused.
You have to expect loud noises and feeling like
your life is actually in danger and feeling like
you're not good enough to pretend to be a soldier
even if they lived hundreds of years ago.
You have to listen to the officers as if
your real life depends on it. You can't worry
about losing your boyfriend.
You can worry about dying
even if it's only pretend.

When going to battle
you have to live in each second.
Each shout.
You can't look for your friends
in the crowd of onlookers.

You have to stare straight ahead.
At the enemies.

HOW TO DIE

I cheat and die the same time as you.
I wonder what you're thinking about—
if you invent
a reason or a story
as you find a moment to fall.

I wish I was more in the moment
but all I can think about

is the real-life
me and you who still have
so much life to live—
I wonder if our soldiers were
as scared as we are.

Maybe they were even more scared
someone would discover
they were trans if they died
in battle or after
the war was over
and they had to go back to
the towns they were from.

I hope our soldiers
survived the battle to figure it out.

It's customary that
first-time reenactors die first,
so our death was predetermined

but it still feels heavy.

GHOSTS

We talk to each other
while lying there.

You inch closer to me
and rest your head
on my shoulder.

You shout over
the cannon fire,
"I love the name David!

That man we stood next to,
that's his 'colonial' name."

"That's funny cis people
pick names for reenacting," I say.
"Do you not like Oliver, though?"

"No, I love Oliver, sometimes
I just wish I could have more than
one name."

"Middle name?" I ask.

You nod. "Yes! Why didn't
I think of that?
We get middle names!"

The ground rumbles with
another round of cannon fire.

"I'm scared that if I add a name or pick a new name
that people will think I'm not sure
about being trans,"
I say.

You shrug. "People will think a lot of things."

STONE

On my gravestone I hope
they put the right name. I think about this the
whole time we're talking. I feel bad for pretending
to be dead when people actually really did die on the grass
where I am . . . maybe they can feel me. Maybe they like the
company, maybe they look up and think about how
warm   our   bodies   are,
how young we are, how our shoes step carefully across the earth.
I want to tell you that I might change my name again but that
seems too wishy-washy. I mean, I already put
everyone through the
trouble of calling me one thing and now I'm not even sure if
that's right. I feel really sad. I don't always feel sad
in places like graveyards
but this time I do. I feel so sad. The ground under me is hard
and it feels like it's getting harder—turning to stone.
I want to cry, not for any reason other than just to let
something out,
I don't know what.
I'm tired. I was up too late, that's why, maybe. I'm thinking
I should tell you, I should but I already am, my mouth is open,

"I DIDN'T GET INTO SCHOOL YET,"

I say, and you roll over on your side,
your uniform and face smudged
with soot and mud.

You hold my hand.
Yours is cold.

Mine is warm.

282

I keep thinking you're going
to say something but you don't.

You just pet my hand
and put your arm around me.

I wonder if any of the soldiers
notice us but when I look
I see their rows moving
forward.

They're making ground!

At least our side
is winning

and will win.

"WHY DIDN'T YOU TELL ME?"

You take a long time to ask
and you do between bursts of musket fire.
I'm glad you take a long time because
it gives me time to put together
all my thoughts. Everything I'm going
to say to you about how sorry I am
and how I should have just said
I got wait-listed and how I should
have trusted you not to judge me
for not having a plan for next year yet.
You keep the same posture, stroking my hand.
I remember envisioning something different
for this whole trip. I imagined getting to redo
how winter break was supposed to be, like
summer all over again. Like the hill where
we both smelled like fresh-cut grass. I run
a hand through your hair. I'm sorry.

WANDERING

I imagine our soldiers' souls

rising from their bodies. I imagine us

walking through the debris of the quiet field.

You say, "It's okay not to know what you're doing,

    at least that's what my mom keeps repeating but it
        never feels like it's true.

        I feel like everyone expects us to know exactly
           where we want

           to be in ten years. I don't even know
              what I'll look like in ten years

           or if I'll take hormones or have
              surgery or if I'll have none

           of that and I'll figure out the trans
              thing another way.

        I guess what I mean is that it's okay and art
           school is

        hard. I guess I'm also like, really? You're the
           best artist I know.

        Try next year if this year it doesn't work out.

        Am I rambling? I'm always rambling. I hope
           we like

           still talk in college and stuff. I need
              you."

    I sigh. "You're going to make all sorts of new college
        friends."

You frown. "I can have new friends and still love you. You can meet them!"

"Yeah, I know," I say.

I take note of the other soldiers pretending to be dead.

I pretend I'm recalling them. "Alexander," I say. "He and his lover ran a bakery in town." You follow my lead.

"Daniel, he made his own chest binder, reshaping

a really tight corset. A visionary. Ahead of his time."

We laugh and I feel so much better that I don't have to think about telling you anymore.

WHEREVER YOU'RE BURIED

Dear Aaron,

My name is also Aaron.

I named myself after you.

Wherever you're buried

whether or not we find evidence of you

I want you to know that you

matter to me.

I think about your life still.

You made me care about history.

You made me think that I'll have a history,

which is hard to remember when

everything in the moment is so much.

I often feel like I want to be a boy

and then I remember that I am one.

Can you give me some of your boyness?

Your old ties?

Your tricks on how to grow up

when no one sees you as you?

I don't know who Oliver

was to you but I have an Oliver, too.

He's beautiful.

I love you

more than you could ever know.

I wish I could have loved you

when you were alive.

The thought of seeing you

is like you dying all over again.

I love you.

—Aaron

NIGHT

We're exhausted after
the battle even though
it only lasted about three hours.

The men in charge all congratulated us
on our uniforms and how well
we followed orders.

I can tell this made you proud.

They say they're so happy
such young boys are interested
in living history.

We lie down early
on our sleeping
bags even though
other people are still meandering around
the tent area.

In my sleeping bag
I write the letter to him

while you stare up
at another sunset.

"I'm writing him a letter," I say
to get your attention.

Cerise and Acacia are at their tent
checking inventory
after a day of sales.

You look at me.
"Can I tell you something?"

"Sure."

"I got a text from my mom."

I look up from writing.
"Yeah?"

"She's mad about all this."

I nod. "I'm sorry."

". . . She said she has to tell your mom
when we get back."

I feel my face flush,
so angry I can feel it in my teeth.

"Why the fuck would she do that?"

"She said it's not right to keep
things from other parents.
Not until we get back.
I'm sorry. I shouldn't
have told you."

"My parents will literally handcuff me to
my bed and pray with rosaries over me.
Why would she fucking do that?"
You flip over and lie on your back.
"I'm sorry, Aaron, I don't know.
I just thought it'd be shitty not
to tell you."

"This is fucking stupid,
this whole trip was stupid," I say even though
I don't really mean it.

I grab my uniform coat and trample out
away from the field

with the letter in my hand,
all crumpled up.

"Hey, wait!" you say, sitting up
as I start running.

I know its dumb and dramatic to leave

but I have to.

I feel this rushing need
to escape everything,
even this fake reenactment world

we spent the past two days in.
There has to be
someplace else.

AWAY FROM EVERYTHING

Really, I'm not even that mad.
I'm just scared
and all the strangeness hits me:
the sadness of it all,
the reality of how far we are
from everything we know.
The colors are even different.
My clothing is a uniform.
Am I really at war?
Is this really 1778?
I run and run.
The woods get thicker.
Out of habit I turn to my phone
and remember I don't have service here.
I just want to get lost on Instagram

or Twitter or something.
I feel like this is the last night
I'll ever get to feel like this.
I imagine the way my mother's face
will twist up when she sees me,
that kind of disappointed look
only moms can make. What's worse
is I actually feel like I'm betraying them,
not just for leaving but for
not being their daughter.
I wish I could find a small town
here in the woods
and pretend I'm a different boy.
My name is Mateo, like
my grandfather, that's
what I tell myself.
A totally different boy.
I live here now in this city
of cabins and stones.
I belong here.
I belong here.
I belong here
away from everything.

A ROOM

I wonder if you're following me.
Can you see my path
through the trees?
We know each other like that.
You might feel
where I'm going.
What if you don't?

What if I run
and I'm never
going to make it out of
these woods?
What if that was
the last time I saw you?
It feels terrible
to test you like this,
to see if you'll follow me.
I don't know what I'm doing.
I'm running even though
I haven't realized it till now.
The night is cool.
I feel my whole body.
I feel every inhale,
every muscle,
every joint.
I have such a body.
My heart pounding in my ears.
I think about winter break again,
how badly I wanted a place
for me and you to just
lie together.
Why don't parents let
teenagers do that?
Everyone's always fucking
in cars and back rooms
and alleyways.
Why can't someone just
make a magical room
that we can go to
and be totally alone
with people we want

to learn how to love
body to
body
to body?

I WANT

you and all of you.
It's strange how this hits me
with such force as I'm somewhat
lost jogging between
trees so much
older than us.

I want you so much
and I wonder what that means
when people in movies say "I want you."
I don't just want your body.
I want "us" together with nothing nothing nothing
in the way.

I feel bad
that I'm thinking about having
sex with you in the woods.

That's weird,
right?
I don't know whether
or not I'll tell you about these thoughts.

I don't even know if you'll
find me.

I realize that the woods
get deeper and darker and denser
the farther I go.

And then they're thinning again.
It looks like
there's a clearing
ahead.

Everything is shadow
and I'm afraid to be alone
and I believe I just
need to get there

to the clearing
and there I'll be safe.

GRAVES

At first,
they look like
tree stumps

in rows in the clearing.

I get closer,
panting,
sweating,
crying.

I kneel.

They're tombstones.

Yes.

In the woods?

Maybe old.
Maybe Revolutionary War era.

Could they be?

I touch the cool stone.

The lettering is worn
and almost illegible
but I make out the year on this first one

1778

WHEN YOU FIND ME

it's probably an hour later.
Maybe it was less.
I don't know time anymore.

You don't say my name.
You know it's me.

I feel a guilt rush over me
for not just taking
a walk with you to talk about things,
for not using words,
for just running away into
these woods.

You wrap your arms around me,
hugging me from behind.

I cry and you cry.

"Do you understand?" you ask.

"What?"
I'm confused.

"These are their graves," you say.

"Whose?" I say.

"Our soldiers,
our soldiers whose names
we can't find. They're gone
like the names
on these tombstones.
But they're here!"

"It doesn't make a difference to me
if we ever find real proof of
trans soldiers in the Revolution.
Think of how
many stories no one will know.
Just 'cause they're unknown stories
doesn't mean they're any less real."

"I'm sorry about my mom,"
you say, tearing up again.

"I know," I say. "I know
you're sorry.
I still shouldn't have acted
ridiculously like that."

You smile and repeat,
"It's okay, it's okay.

We'll get through this," you say,

and I believe you.

NO ONE

No one else in the entire world
is actually there anymore.

It's just you and me
in this graveyard.

Maybe even all the graves beneath us
are empty.

Maybe they're part of the dirt
and the grass
and the roots and
the lush green summer leaves.

Calming down, I notice the glow
of lightning bugs all around and remember
the lightning bugs
in town,

how we'd spend hours
catching them and
letting them go.

I want to catch
the lights and let them go.

You cup one in your hand
and say,
"It's for you."

I kiss your ear.

You let the firefly go.

EARS

When I kiss your
ear you flinch and laugh.

"Is that okay?" I ask.

"Yeah, you just never did that before. I like it."

I kiss your ear slower this time.

All the little hairs
on your neck stand up.

We haven't kissed like this
in so long.

Until now there's been
this drifting distance between us

and I'm scared if I don't
keep kissing you
that it will come back

and I'll feel far away
from you again.

I've heard people tell horror stories
about kissing with too much tongue
or not enough

and I feel lucky because
I've only ever kissed you and
kissing you is smooth
and soft like eating canned peaches.

You kiss my neck.
I kiss yours.

We go back and forth with our movements,
trading touches.

"Do you think anyone
will see us here?" you ask.

"I don't think so," I say.

"I don't want to get in trouble," you say,
"but I don't think it's that big a deal even
if someone came here."

"Tomorrow's our last day here," I say.

You smile and kiss me more.

I kiss your neck and you
let out a soft moan.

"Bite it," you say, "bite my neck,"

which startles me
because I'm not sure how hard
and I don't know anything about being sexy.

"How hard?" I ask.

"It's okay, I'll let you know,
would you want to try it?"

SOIL

I love the smell of earth.

You climb down
on the ground first
and I laugh from nervousness
and because it's ridiculous
and because I want to lose my virginity in a graveyard.

Dad used to till the small plot
behind the house for his garden
each late March.
That's what the dirt reminds me of,
standing barefoot next to you while
I showed you how to pluck
the cherry tomatoes from their plants.

"Can I take this off?" I ask,
touching your back underneath
your shirt.

"Please," you say, and I do
and you take off mine

and the ground is soft and hard
and you move on top of me

both of us with underwear still on,
humping gently, then faster.

"Can I get on top of you?" you ask,
and I nod, noticing how fast
we're both breathing.

You touch me over
my underwear.

You laugh

and I ask, "What?"

"Nothing."

"No really, what?"

"I wish I had a dick with me."

I laugh. "I do too."

We slow down for a second,
your hand still touching softly between
my legs.

"What do you want me to call it?"

"You can call it my dick,
I like that," I say. "What do I call yours?"

"I don't mind calling mine
a vagina, do you think that's okay?" you ask.

"It's whatever you want,
it's your body," I say.

You keep rubbing me.

"I love touching your dick,"
you say.

I can barely talk.
My face is flushing.
"I love it too,
can I touch you?"

GRASS

The grass is prickly
on my bare skin.
It brushes me every time we turn over.

The tombstones provide just enough cover
so that if someone else were passing
the cemetery they wouldn't even notice us.

Kissing, touching, moving.
I wonder how many things I haven't
seen that were so close to plain sight.

"Can I put my fingers inside you?" you ask.

I take your hand and kiss it over and over.
"I don't think I want anything inside me.
I like what we're doing," I say as
you move on top of me.

"I want you inside me," you say,
"if you want to."

"I do, I do, tell me what feels good,"
and I take one finger then two then three
in slow
you're so warm
and soft and strong.

"I want to make you come," I say.

"I want to make you come too,"
you say,

and I shake my head. "No you, no you."
But you're barely hearing me anymore.

You grip my shoulders
and move slower and more rigidly,
shaking as you come,
closing your eyes,
opening your mouth, and
I want to kiss you more and more.

You lie on my chest,
all our warmness all over each other.

"I love you," I say.

You pinch my arm. "LOL, that's so cliché."

"What? I was serious."

"You only want me for the sex," you tease, rolling over.

I kiss your shoulder.

"Yeah, that's it, Oliver."

"Aaron?"

"What?"

"We just . . . in a cemetery."

"There are probably weirder places," I say.

"Is that like disrespectful?" you ask.

I shrug. "I don't think anyone here
will ever know . . .
I mean, they're dead."

That makes you laugh.

THE LAST DAY IN 1778

We spent the whole night together
in the wood's clearing,

ambling back to our sleeping bags
in the bluish dawn.

You point this out
on the fresh morning walk
and I admit it too,
that I think it was
more romantic
that we lost our virginities
in a graveyard
than in a hotel
or a car
or a bed.

"It's straight out of paranormal romance," you say.
"What would you have done, Aaron, if zombies
had just started popping up?"

"Well, I would have, of course, started
fighting the zombies. I wouldn't want
to be one of those teens who dies in a horror
movie because they're having sex
in the wrong place."

"You would have to protect me,
I'd be useless," you say.

"That's not true,
someone needs to keep up morale
in those movies."

We're too tired from being up
late the night before
to be part of the battle today.

We talk about the future,
for real now, though,
as we get breakfast
from one of the food vendors
(definitely not period-accurate):
hash browns
and a breakfast sandwich.

I tell you how scared I am that
I won't ever do anything with my art

and you tell me how scared you
are that people at your new school
will just be more people who
see you as a girl
instead of the boy you are.

ONE DANCE

With Cerise and Acacia
we walk to the barn where there's a dance.

We're in our uniforms,
which are still slightly dirty
from the battle.

"We're ghosts," we say
to them

and they laugh and say
they're ghosts too
but only because they think
lesbians would make
cute ghosts.

The music is
old-timey—kinda like a folk band.

It's not like prom would have been
but it's so much better.

I can't believe
I'm actually nervous
to slow-dance with you
but you make me less nervous

as we both fumble around
trying to figure out
how to hold each other
and move
with the music.

Cerise takes a picture
of us and sends it to me—

you're mid-laugh
and I'm just smiling
and looking

at you.

BEFORE WE GO

Cerise and Acacia
and you and me
have a big group hug
outside the barn.

We're all kind of gross
and sweaty.

Which reminds me
how super freaking gross
it must have been during the real Revolution
without any showers.

Cerise says, "We're all starting
a blog together.
You two have no choice.
You're stuck with us for good."

"Me?" I ask,
because you're the one
who knows history stuff.
I'd love to do art for it
but I'm not sure if I can write
blog posts.

"Uhhh, of course, Aaron—
we need all of us!" Cerise says.
"I've decided it now, we'll trade off

writing posts about queer history
every week."

"Ha-ha—whoa there.
Are you assigning us homework?" Acacia teases.

"You bet I am!" Cerise says.

"I want to write the first post, actually,"
I hear myself say.

"Oh, wow, that's awesome!
What do you want to write about?" you ask.

"Keith Haring, this awesome gay artist
from Kutztown," I say.

"That's perfect, Aaron! I'll tell you what,
I'll pay for the website domain
once you make it, Oliver," Cerise says,
holding out her phone
and instructing us
to write our emails down.

"We're really doing this," you say,
beaming in the glow of the barn light.

"Now all we need is a snappy title," Acacia says.

"What about
Queer-istory?" Cerise says, but before
anyone can say anything
she says, "No, no, that's stupid.
Hmmm, what about
Queer and Now?
Queerly Yours? Queering History?
Queer Quests in History? No, too specific—"

"What about
Queer Revolutions?" you say,

and everyone agrees
that's the one.

SLEEPING

We're too tired
to change into pajamas
after the dance,
so we just lie together.

I'm going to miss our field.

You fall asleep first
like you always do.

I wonder if we'll still love
each other like this if our bodies change
because of hormones or whatever
else we might decide we need
as we get older.

I know now
after all of this
that I want those things,
which scares me.

I make a plan in my head
to search for LGBT clinics
in the city when I get home.

I wonder if my mom texted me.

How mad she'll be at me.

If she'll ever see me as her son.

BACK TO REALITY

Your mom is picking us up
because there's no reason anymore
to keep up the lie that we spent this weekend
at the beach.

I feel bad she drove
all the way here
but it's sure cheaper
than taking an Uber again.

I'm nervous to see your mom
and worried that she'll not
want me to be your friend/boyfriend anymore.

HOME

We're going home, then?
I'm going home and you're going home.

We sit far apart, not touching,
in the back seat of your mom's station wagon.

She's not short with us or upset.
She asks questions
as if the trip to the reenactment was all
planned with her.

"What did you eat?"
"What did you see?"
"Who did you meet?"

She seems genuinely curious
and upbeat,
happy to see us again.

I wonder when that will end.
Even though I love your mom
I know there has to be a point
where this breaks down.

THIS DOESN'T ALL BREAK DOWN

She offers for me to stay the night.
"Aaron, would you be comfortable staying tonight?"

"Really?" I ask, convinced this
is where she tells us how much trouble we're in
and that she's going to drive me right up to New York.
"It's a far drive from here to my house.
I can find my own way back home.
There's another bus to the city tonight I could take."

"Is that what you want?" she asks me.

"No, I'm kind of scared to go back."

"We'll make sure you call your mom
and I can even take you back
tomorrow instead."

"That's so much driving," I say.

"You both just graduated.
It's a small thing," she says.

I shift in the seat, trying to
work up the courage
to ask your mom
if she's told my parents about the trip yet.

I'm happy you ask instead.

"Mom, did you betray Aaron and
tell his parents about where we were yet?"

"No . . . I'm honestly not sure how to.
We even talked on the phone today."

I'm so confused. Your mom?
Talking to my parents?

"Wait, what? You never hung out
with the Solteros much before," you say.

"Well, I wanted to talk to them about
you two, and besides, we've texted for years."

"Years? Us two?" you ask. "You mean us dating?"

"No no no," she said. "I wanted to
talk about . . . well, actually, just about you, Oliver."

"What were you saying?"

"I'm sorry, baby, I know this is awkward."
She glances back at us.

"No, come on, tell me," you say.

"Well, I haven't talked to someone else
with a trans kid, and I just kind of wanted
to talk to someone else about that."

My heart drops.
Sure, I've told my parents, but
that was months ago and no one really
acknowledged it. I just decided
then not to bring it up again.
I still feel like I'm in the closet
because they still treat me like
their daughter—maybe they think

310

they can remind me what being a girl
is like and then I'll change my mind.

Maybe they're scared of what this
means for us.

Sometimes it makes me feel like
I wish I was easier
to take care of—that I was a normal boy
like José.

She glances back again,
worry on her face, "I'm sorry, Aaron,
is that okay?"

"Why did you do that?" you ask.

I'm crying and I wipe my face.
I have been crying sooo much lately.
"No, it's actually really good, like
maybe with you talking they'll start
to see me like that."

"It's hard, Aaron, it's hard."

"But it's hard for him, too," you say.

Your mom nods. "Yes, of course,
you deserve to be seen for who you are.
I think they understand, though."

YOUR HOUSE

Being back in your house makes
me feel like a ghost.

This all feels like another life,
this town where I grew up.

Your mom sets me up
in the attic on the bottom bunk
of the bunk bed

and you ask to stay on
the top bunk.

She gives you
a look and you know that means
not to push it.

Before we go to bed, though,
we hang out in your room like we used to.
You have more records now and
you play a new Lady Gaga one,
which sounds strange coming
from the record player.

You say, "You should check your email,
to see if you heard from any schools."

I think that there's no way there are
any updates.

ACCEPTED

Before I really know what's happening,
you're hugging me.

I say, "What, what?"

"You got in!" you say.

And I say, "No, no, stop, no, I didn't,"
even though the email says:

Congratulations, [****] Soltero,

We're in the process of removing you from the wait list. You need to notify us as soon as possible if you intend to accept this offer to join our program at Pratt for Fine Arts . . .

and I stop reading because that's
all I need to know right now.

I cry for a while,
and all of a sudden

I need to be with my parents,

I want to be with them right now,
but I don't tell you that.

I let you hold me
and I live right now with you

and I feel like
I wouldn't change anything
about us

and I say a prayer
to Oliver and Aaron, as if they
were our saints,

and I know that
somewhere
and somehow they know
that we exist
as much as we know they do.

PHONE CALL

It's late at night
but I call Mom and Dad anyway.

"Hi," I say, nervously.
God, I'm like almost shaking.

"[****]? No—I mean Aaron.
Aaron?" Mom asks.

I cry.

She's never said
my name before.

"Are you okay?" she asks.

"I'm more than okay," I say.
"I got in—I really got in
to college."

She screams
so loud and excited
I have to move the phone away
from my face.

I haven't heard her
so excited
maybe since before we moved.

"We're having a party—
we need to have a party," she says.
"Let me get Dad—"

I hear her voice
slightly muffled
in the background.

She says, "Luis! Luis, [****] got in to college."

I can't hear what Dad says
but he sounds excited.

I know more is coming—
Mom's not just going to let me get off easy
after I literally broke like every possible rule:
running away,
lying,
AND not texting her back.

She comes back to the phone
and clears her throat.
"That's such good news, baby . . .

You do know
you're VERY grounded."

I sigh, kind of relieved actually
to be talking to Mom
and that she's not so mad that
she won't talk to me anymore.

There's a pause on the line.
I'm thinking about how
for the first time since I left

I want to be home.

I want to be with them.

She says, "I'm sorry, baby.
I know this is hard. I wish
I'd understood earlier.
Really, I was hoping
this was some phase—
not because it's such a bad thing
but because I don't want your life
to be so hard.
Do you understand what I mean?
I worried you were doing it for attention—

to rebel or something.
Damn! And that sounds bad.
What I'm trying to say is—"

I hear the phone rustle as Dad takes it.
"We love you," Dad says.
"And it's true you've always been
a little more macho anyway, right?"

"Yes—yes, and
we'll be here for you
as our son," Mom adds.

I sigh, cradling the phone.
I know it's not the most like correct thing to say—
being "macho" or more masculine
doesn't automatically make someone a man—
but coming from Dad it feels
so affirming.

I worried he might never get it.

I don't know what to say.
I just hold the phone—
wishing we were all together
in the living room,
Mom cooking something for dinner
with a baseball game on the TV.

"I just want you guys to listen to me," I say.

And I don't think
I could have said that
a week ago.

It's like all the energy
of the battle drums and the fireflies

and the thick humid June night
poured into me.

She says, "I will.
We will.
I promise."
She pauses before adding,
"And YOU have
to promise not to lie to me!"

"I won't—I won't."

"You bet you won't,"
Mom says
with a hint of softness.

I stand there
alone for a moment—
imagining new family pictures
and a party with my whole family
where everyone calls me
Aaron.

I hang up the phone
and sneak back
down the hall
to your room,

where you're asleep
and the only light

is the moon
round and full
through your open window.

JUNE 1778, A WEEK BEFORE THE BATTLE OF MONMOUTH

Dear Oliver,

I'm thinking about you
and those cold nights this winter.

I'm writing to you,
even though I know you could
be dead.

I'm talking to you,
even though I know I might
never see you again.

I pray one of these nights
I'll meet you in the woods,
even if it's just your ghost.

Because I believe that I have loved you,
Oliver. I have.

I have truly,
and no one but us will ever know
our truths.

I love you. I love you. I love you.

—Aaron

Dear Aaron,

I'm thinking about you,
and the depth and darkness
and beauty of the Pennsylvanian forest.

I'm writing to you,
even though I know we might never
find each other.

Even though I know
after this we might never get
to be the men we are again.

I'm talking to you,
even though you could be gone.

Because I believe that I have loved you,
Aaron. I have.

I have truly,
and I worry no one will love
like this again.

How will they know we existed
without any evidence?

I love you. I love you. I love you.

—Oliver

AUTHOR'S NOTE

Hi there. This is Robin, the author of this book. I wanted to give you a little bit of background about Oliver and Aaron and their soldiers. I started writing *A Million Quiet Revolutions* with the goal of writing a love story I would have wanted as a teenager before I came out. In high school and middle school, I often had moments of realization that I wasn't cisgender (*cisgender* meaning "not trans"), but I didn't have the words to articulate being a trans person. Honestly, I didn't fully understand that trans people existed. I grew up in Kutztown, the town where Oliver and Aaron's story begins, and there is a lot of beauty there, but also a lot of isolation for a queer person. I never saw love stories that involved genderqueer, gender-nonconforming, or transgender people, especially not between trans people. My history classes likewise never covered gay rights or any trans or queer history. Still, I was always curious.

In fifth grade, I remember learning about female soldiers dressing as men to be part of the Revolution. I was fascinated by this idea even then, and at recess sometimes when we played "war" (which has its own issues, but let's not unpack that now), I would pretend to be one of those soldiers. I think back then I was so drawn to this knowledge because it was evidence that gender was not fixed; it showed that people had been crafting their own genders for centuries.

It is very hard to assign people from the past labels that we use today. I think this is something we should see as exciting and not discouraging. Evolving and changing language around gender identity is evidence that our gender identities have also always been evolving and changing. There have always been people who resist the constraints of gender norms and assigned genders.

Though there is no specific documentation to support the love story of the two soldiers from this book, there is evidence that some female soldiers continued to live as men after the Revolutionary War. However, I firmly believe the story is true. How can we queer people trust a history, which was mostly reported and documented by cisgender people, to present our joy, our love, and our flourishing? Right now there are a lot of really amazing queer historians doing this work, and you should check them out, but I also think it is an important radical act to imagine wherever we might have existed beyond what research has uncovered. Personally, my philosophy behind this book is that it is not a question of whether trans and queer people have existed throughout history. It is a question of who is telling their stories, if their stories are being told at all. If you'd like to know more, I invite you to take a look at these resources and books by some queer and trans historians, writers, and artists. I want to add, if you ever can't find information you're looking for, don't let that limit your imagination and curiosity about history. History is something everyone can and should explore and critique no matter their age or experience. This list is in no way complete but it might be somewhere to start. Outside of books and websites, there are also zines, blogs, Twitter and Instagram accounts, and all kinds of content creators telling stories of trans and queer history, so always keep searching.

WEBSITES

GLSEN LGBTQ History: https://www.glsen.org/lgbtq-history
History UnErased: https://unerased.org

FURTHER READING
ON TRANS*, GENDER-NONCONFORMING, AND TWO-SPIRIT PEOPLE'S HISTORY

Asegi Stories: Cherokee Queer and Two-Spirit Memory by Qwo-Li Driskill

Bad Indians: A Tribal Memoir by Deborah A. Miranda

Becoming a Visible Man by Jamison Green

Black on Both Sides: A Racial History of Trans Identity by C. Riley Snorton

Bordered Lives: Transgender Portraits from Mexico by Kike Arnal

Borderlands/La Frontera: The New Mestiza by Gloria Anzaldúa

Brilliant Imperfection: Grappling with Cure by Eli Clare

Captive Genders: Trans Embodiment and the Prison Industrial Complex edited by Eric A. Stanley and Nat Smith, foreword by CeCe McDonald

Crip Theory: Cultural Signs of Queerness and Disability by Robert McRuer

Female Husbands: A Trans History by Jen Manion

Female Masculinity by Jack Halberstam

How Sex Changed: A History of Transsexuality in the United States by Joanne Meyerowitz

Mobile Subjects: Transnational Imaginaries of Gender Reassignment by Aren Z. Aizura

Moving Truth(s): Queer and Transgender Desi Writings on Family edited by Aparajeeta Duttchoudhury and Rukie Hartman

Normal Life: Administrative Violence, Critical Trans Politics, and the Limits of Law by Dean Spade

Queer, There, and Everywhere: 23 People Who Changed the World by Sarah Prager

Queer Ricans: Cultures and Sexualities in the Diaspora edited by Lawrence La Fountain-Stokes

Real Queer America: LGBT Stories from Red States by Samantha Allen

Redefining Realness: My Path to Womanhood, Identity, Love & So Much More by Janet Mock

Re-Dressing America's Frontier Past by Peter Boag

Sex Changes: Transgender Politics by Patrick Califia

Sister Outsider: Essays and Speeches by Audre Lorde

The Men with the Pink Triangle: The True Life-and-Death Story of Homosexuals in the Nazi Death Camps by Heinz Heger

The Right to Be Out: Sexual Orientation and Gender Identity in America's Public Schools by Stuart Biegel

The Stonewall Reader by the New York Public Library, foreword by Edmund White

The Truth About Me: A Hijra Life Story by A. Revathi

Through the Door of Life: A Jewish Journey between Genders by Joy Ladin

Tomorrow Will Be Different: Love, Loss, and the Fight for Trans Equality by Sarah McBride, forword by Joe Biden

Trans*: A Quick and Quirky Account of Gender Variability by Jack Halberstam

Trans Exploits: Trans of Color Cultures and Technologies in Movement by Jian Neo Chen

Transgender History: The Roots of Today's Revolution by Susan Stryker

Transgender and Jewish edited by Naomi Zeveloff

Transgender Warriors: Making History from Joan of Arc to Dennis Rodman by Leslie Feinberg

True Sex: The Lives of Trans Men at the Turn of the 20th Century by Emily Skidmore

Sovereign Erotics: A Collection of Two-Spirit Literature edited by Qwo-Li Driskill, Daniel Heath Justice, Deborah Miranda, and Lisa Tatonetti

We Are Everywhere: Protest, Power, and Pride in the History of Queer Liberation by Matthew Riemer and Leighton Brown

We Have Always Been Here: A Queer Muslim Memoir by Samra Habib

When Brooklyn Was Queer by Hugh Ryan

ACKNOWLEDGMENTS

I have first the trans community to thank for this book. Sometimes saying "the trans community" feels too impossibly vast to name because trans people are so diverse and unique but I want to name the community here to acknowledge how the myriad of trans experiences ignited and fed this book. I'm grateful especially to the GSA at Ursinus College and Institute for Inclusion and Equity for giving me space to embrace my gender and my queerness. Special gratitude to Terrence Williams and Patrick Robinson there.

I'm indebted to the dozens of trans people I've met through Trans-cendent Connections and the Philly Trans Wellness Conference. The experiences and education you share impact the lives of trans youth across the country and gave me a sense of home and family when I was first coming out.

Thank you, Jordan Hamessley, my agent, for believing in this book and my poetry in its very early and complicated stages. I'm forever grateful for the time you took to work with me revising this story and, in the process, bringing out Oliver and Aaron's love story even more.

So many thanks to my editor, Trisha de Guzman, who shaped this story in more ways than can be counted. Each revision was a joy because of how deeply you understood and celebrated these characters' journeys.

To Michelle Bermudez, thank you for your time and thoughtful reading of this book. Your reflections guided the story toward its conclusion and I couldn't have found it alone. Your own poetry is stunning and vital.

I want to thank my MFA cohort at Adelphi University (Gina,

Benny, Lex, Nicole, Nii, Barbara, and Michael) for reading and workshopping a very early draft of this book, and our professor, Donna Freitas, without whom I wouldn't have even tried my hand at writing a YA novel. When I first entered Donna's class I knew basically nothing about YA—her brilliant teaching opened me up to a world of literature I now adore and her friendship is a blessing.

Special thanks to my friends Jey, Solana, Ben, Joe, Paige, Ryan, Frozen, Benny, Rachel, and Kat, who are there for me as a writer and as a queer and trans person. You're all brilliant creative humans I'm so lucky to know. My heart will always be with you, my chosen family. And thank you to my partner Saturn for being my home and my light.

I'm also indebted to my English and creative writing professors throughout the years, who nurtured me as a person as well as a writer. There's not enough space to thank everyone adequately but I owe who I am as a poet to Jacqueline Jones Lamon, Judith Baumel, M. Nzadi Keita, Anna Maria Hong, and Jon Volkmer and I'm also grateful to professors at Ursinus College: Meredith Goldsmith, Patti Schroeder, Rebecca Jaroff, Matthew Kozusko, Kara McShane, Meghan Brodie, and Abby Kluchin, for their mentorship, encouragement, and open office doors. Thank you to the writing community at Ursinus College, especially Lit Soc, for inspiring me to want to write better poems to bring to each week's meeting.

From Kutztown, I want to thank my high school friends: Karl, Alex, Katie, Jocelyn, Catie, and Ness for sharing those complicated yet often beautiful times with me. I want to thank my teachers Mrs. Saby, Mr. Chambers, Mrs. Chester, Mrs. Westgate, Mrs. Hall, Mrs. Boyer, and Mrs. Howard, whose classrooms were my havens, and Firefly Book Store, whose poetry open mics were the highlights of my months senior year. Also a thank-you to the Young Readers Young Writers Program for embracing me as a young storyteller, especially Mr. Hartle.

Last but not least, I need to thank my parents for always reading to me and encouraging my creativity and my brothers for being the first people I told stories with. My brother Billy was the one who introduced me to the world of reenacting and his stories inspired these characters' interests and curiosities.